THE
MALLORCAN
GAMBIT

THE MALLORCAN GAMBIT

JUDITH FABRIS
SHARON PRIETO
DONNA WEEKS

SUNACUMEN
PRESS

ISBN: 979-8-9914967-9-7

Published by Sunacumen Press
Colorado Springs, CO
Printed in the U.S.A.

PROLOGUE

The night was pitch black as her old BMW wound down the treacherous mountain road. The switchbacks forced her to rapidly alternate between pressing the gas and stomping on the brake, as she navigated the rapid descent. She held the steering wheel in a death grip until her hands ached and her body shook.

She couldn't stop thinking of the torture she would have to endure if sent to prison. She'd heard stories.

But what an exit!

Be warned.
Soon one of you will die and another will stand trial for murder.

She prayed neither would apply to her.

Speeding as though chased by the devil, she ignored the warm wetness between her legs as her bladder found release. She must not be caught.

Bright lights coming at her fast caused her to pull hard right and the Beemer flew around an S-curve. Stabbing pain raced up her left side, as her ribs connected with the door handle. Overcorrecting, she slid halfway to the opposite door, nearly losing her grip on the steering wheel. Bright lights blinded her, and confused, she again pulled to the left, barely avoiding a head-on collision.

The scene through her windshield now revealed nothing but darkness — no curves, no bright lights. The road seemed much smoother here, but the car was going down too fast, like a roller coaster on the straightaway. Then she felt light as though flying. The world slowed.

Abruptly, the hood turned down and vomit spewed from her gaping mouth as the car flipped, the shattered windshield spraying glass. The BMW landed hard on its roof and slid with a deafening metallic screech, into the bottom of a deep ravine.

The world went dark.

CHAPTER 1

Earlier that evening

A slight sensation of unease blanketed the room, like the icy fingers of creeping fog.

The room was small and dark, illuminated by tiny, twinkling lights over an unlit fireplace and three white candles on the long, rectangular table. The scent of cinnamon wafted lightly through the space, as intonations of Benedictine monks provided ghostly chanting for the occasion. Though nine people were seated, there was no conversation.

"Where is she? I expected her to be here to greet us," grumbled one man finally, looking at his watch impatiently.

"Let's give her a few minutes," offered one of the women. "I'm sure she has everything prepared. We're in no hurry."

"From what I hear, she's drop-dead gorgeous and single

... a chick well worth waiting for," snarked a guy with questionable motives for being there. "I hear she looks exactly like Halle Berry."

Time passed. The atmosphere of curiosity was overlaid with a hint of desperation.

The group was a mix of people — old, young, married, single — each there with a different expectation.

A tall, slim, grey-haired professorial type, Arthur Webster, bore a faint resemblance to Alex Trebek.

Roger and Grace Chen, married 23 years, had recently experienced a family tragedy.

A twenty-something man wearing a neon green golf shirt, Lance Harris, was a student at the local community college.

Brad Merrill, the slick man who had commented earlier on the host's appearance, made no pretense of being there for any other reason than to hit on the medium. He appeared to be of mixed race, ruggedly handsome and supremely confident — think Idris Elba, the actor — with an overinflated ego.

A recent arrival from the Midwest, Phiona Beatrice Wahl (Phebe for short) had left a failed relationship and a predictable life in search of a more exciting permanent home. With expertise in the art and theater world, she planned to re-invent herself in the vibrant local community.

Three attractive women of a "certain age" had arrived together — apparently friends, who shared a love of the arts and literature. Their names were Mallory Crawford, Dana Pierce, and Emily Schmidt.

Clearly, a few of the nine participants were skeptics and were either there to support someone else, to pursue an agenda of their own, or simply driven by a sense of curiosity.

The séance was about to begin. Everything was ready. But where was the medium?

Suddenly, the door opened, and a stunningly beautiful woman burst into the room. The three friends had jokingly predicted that the medium would be dumpy, overweight, fifty-ish, with heavy makeup, gaudy jewelry, wearing a muumuu and perhaps, even a turban. In truth, she was a statuesque 5'9", slim and fit, with smooth, golden skin, long flowing black hair flecked with gray, and the biggest lavender eyes imaginable. She didn't fit their stereotype of a medium in any way. On this occasion she looked terrified.

Standing at one end of the table, she announced in a shaky voice, "Tonight there will be no séance. But be warned. Soon, someone in this room will die and another will be charged with murder."

Silence filled the room as the mysterious Annalore Dubois quickly slipped away.

CHAPTER 2

The nine participants froze in their chairs, wondering if the murderer could be sitting right next to them. Suddenly, a metallic screech pierced the silence, accompanied by audible gasps, screams and swearing.

Mrs. Chen cried, "No! No! No!" Her husband pulled her close, as she moaned, "No, no, no more death!"

"Sorry folks. It was just me, pushing my chair back. Relax. I'm not going to kill anyone and I'm not going to wait around to be killed," smirked Brad Merrill, the handsome, roguish man, as he headed toward the door. He continued. "I'm going to find that gorgeous psychic and invite her to have a drink with me. I know she could use a little attention."

Speechless, everyone avoided looking at one another as they pulled themselves together.

Who is this guy? wondered Dana, one of the three friends. *He's dangerously attractive, but clearly full of himself!*

Mallory murmured, "There's a coffee shop about a half-block from here, if anyone is interested." Leaning into her friends, Emily and Dana, she asked if they were ready to leave. They both nodded an emphatic yes, as they gathered their purses. With a smile, Mallory included the woman sitting next to her. Relieved, the stranger grabbed her handbag and hurried to join them. As they walked toward the front door, Mallory invited the remaining people at the table.

"We're going to the coffee shop at the end of the block. Please join us."

Arthur Webster, the older gentleman, picked up a photo lying on the table in front of him and slipped it tenderly into his jacket pocket. He acknowledged Mallory's invitation, as he slid away from the table to follow the women.

The Chens stood and readied themselves to leave. The young man who had been sitting next to them also stood and spoke, saying, "When I arrived tonight, I heard you say your name was 'Chen,' and that your late son had attended the community college in Palm Desert. Was his name 'Roger?' Forgive me, I've forgotten my manners. My name is Lance Harris."

Mr. Chen replied, "Yes. Our son was Roger. Did you know him?"

Lance continued. "Roger was in my writing class at College of the Desert, and I was just getting to know him when he passed away. He was a wonderful guy. I'm so sorry for your loss."

Mrs. Chen began to weep. Her husband put his arms around her in a loving embrace and whispered in her ear. A moment later, he looked at Lance and asked, "Would you join us at the coffee shop?"

"Of course. It would be my pleasure," replied Lance.

The Whimsical Mug was everyone's dream of a quaint coffee shop in a scenic mountain village. Lured in by the strong aroma of freshly brewed coffee, customers were instantly charmed by the ambience of the place. A cluster of comfortable chairs and a brightly colored chintz-covered sofa faced a pot belly stove in one corner. Several small tables and three large booths filled the space. Carefully placed potted plants added an organic sensibility and an old-fashioned soda fountain completed the homey scene.

Two female servers shifted into action as the door opened, letting in the chilly mountain air.

The four women entered, looked around and headed toward one of the booths. Following close behind were Mr. and Mrs. Chen and Lance. They gazed awkwardly around the space and finally opted for the booth next to the four women. They all acknowledged one another as the Chens sat down.

The door opened again, and Arthur Webster entered.

Mallory, who appeared to be the leader of the threesome, called out to him. "Won't you come join us?"

"Thank you," he said.

Mallory introduced herself and her two friends to the other woman. "I'm Mallory and this is Emily," she said, pointing to her friend with salt and pepper, curly hair. "This is Dana," she looked toward the short-haired blond woman. "And you are?"

"I'm Phebe, new to this part of the world," she answered. "Nice to meet you all and thanks for including me. I was, and still am, feeling unnerved!"

The others nodded in agreement, as they began an energetic discussion about the frightening experience.

Suddenly, the entrance door banged open, letting in a blast of cold air, along with the annoying man who had gone looking for the psychic.

"There's not one damn bar open in this hick mountain town. Idyllwild. 'Idyll' is correct; just dump the 'wild' and the name works. I'm going back down the hill to my home in the desert, which has its own bar."

"Sorry. I don't know your name. Did you find the psychic? We're all concerned about her," asked Mallory.

"Just call me Brad, honey, and no, I didn't — not a sign of her. I looked up and down the street and knocked on a couple of doors. Nothing! It's like that old cliché: she's disappeared into thin air!"

With a sigh, Brad looked around the coffee shop for a place to sit.

"How about pushing these tables together so we can talk about what occurred and try to figure out what happened to that beautiful woman tonight? More important, we can discuss who's going to get killed and who the murderer might be, and why." He pointed at Lance.

"Come here. You're young and strong. Give me a hand."

The two got the tables set up quickly, much to the consternation of the waitstaff, who asked, "Coffees all around?"

"Let's get started," Brad began. "Two questions. Who are you and why did you come tonight?"

There was no response.

"It goes like this. I'm Brad Merrill and I came tonight because I wanted to connect with the stunning Annalore Dubois. Next?"

Offended, Mr. Chen stood up and offered his hand to his wife, saying it was time to go. Mrs. Chen took his hand and turned to Lance, thanking him for his kindness. She handed him their business card and asked him to please call them.

Lance rose, shook Mr. Chen's hand, smiled at Mrs. Chen, and offered to walk them to their car. He turned to the group. "I'm a student and I'm leaving too. I have an eight o'clock class tomorrow. My class assignment is to write a report on a new experience. I saw a flyer advertising this séance and thought, why not? It should be an interesting paper, given what happened tonight!"

"You've got that right," said Emily.

The group waved good-bye, then settled down again.

Emily continued. "I'm here with my good friends, Dana and Mallory. We live in the desert, read about this séance, and decided to come to Idyllwild for the experience." She laughed. "Certainly wasn't what we were expecting!"

"Nor I. My name is Arthur Webster. I too, came out of curiosity and in hopes of communicating with my wife, whom I lost recently. I really miss talking to her. She was born in France and her birth name was Martine, but to me she was simply 'Marni.' Her death came as a complete shock and I'm convinced there was something suspicious about it, as she was always in robust health. There are times when I feel quite lost." He paused, reached into his pocket, and removed the photo, placing it on the table.

The room quieted as they passed around the photo.

Phebe held it and said, "Arthur, your wife was beautiful. I know what it is to lose someone you care about. I moved out here after a personal loss, not knowing anyone. I've now met all of you, despite the unsettling circumstances."

The introductions continued.

"My name is Dana and sometimes I feel lost too. Right now, I'd give anything for a large glass of chardonnay to calm my nerves!"

There were smiles as the others agreed enthusiastically.

Emily spoke up. "Like all of you, I'm alarmed by the psychic's prediction. Do any of you really think we're in danger? That one of us is going to be murdered by someone who was there?"

At that moment, the lights in the coffee shop began blinking. There were gasps.

"Relax. There won't be a murder here tonight. We're just closing," the manager called out.

Outdoors, the group began to disperse.

Mallory looked closely at Phebe. "I feel like we've met before."

Phebe slowly began to smile. "Are you *the* Mallory? Hmm. I believe you are. What a surprise! Yes, we do know each other. We met a long time ago in New York. I was Sam Stevens' partner."

"Oh! That's it! I remember now. How are you? How is Sam? What are you doing here? We have to catch up. Do you have a place to stay tonight, or are you headed back down the mountain?"

"I hadn't given it any thought," replied Phebe.

"Why don't you stay with us? We have a suite at the Fireside Lodge with plenty of room for you. We can catch up and try to make some sense out of what just happened. Right, ladies?"

"Yes, Phebe," Dana and Emily chorused. "Please stay with us. We promise you'll be safe and there's definitely a lot more to talk about!"

CHAPTER 3

Thanks to the bitterly cold wind and low temperature, the four women raced up the hill from the coffee shop to the Fireside Lodge. Soon they were in their suite, nestled in comfortable chairs in front of a roaring fire, sipping hot mulled cider — liberally laced with rum, of course — and munching on home-baked chocolate chip cookies, courtesy of Mallory. Dana, true to form, had opted for her favorite chardonnay.

"Brrrrrrr! It's cold outside!" exclaimed Phebe. "I wasn't prepared for this after a 90-degree afternoon in Palm Springs."

"Welcome to our world," laughed Emily. "Since we're all full-time desert rats, we think the weather's cold if it dips below 70!"

On entering the lodge, Mallory had given Phebe a tour of their rooms. The suite included a full kitchen, a cozy living room with tall ceilings, a big stone fireplace and two sofas that doubled as pull-out beds. There was one bed-room with two queen-sized beds and a full bath. While the place wasn't luxurious, it was clean and rustic — a perfect get-away from the desert below.

"Before we start talking about the elephant in the room," Phebe began, "I want to thank you all for making room here for me tonight. I hadn't realized how treacherous it would be driving back to the Valley at night."

"No problem for us," remarked Mallory with a smile. "We happen to have a spare sofa. Since you and I have met before and share interests in the art world, I don't think you'll pose any danger to us!"

Everyone chuckled.

Finally, Dana raised the subject everyone wanted to talk about. "Okay. It's time. What the hell happened tonight at the séance? Does anyone have a clue?"

"I'm as confused as everybody else," said Emily. "That medium, Annalore Dubois, was not what I expected at all. She looked as if she'd stepped off a *Vogue* cover. Did you notice her luminous lavender eyes? I don't know what got into her, but she was absolutely terrified!"

Emily paused a moment and then added, "You know, maybe that jerk, Brad, had the right idea. If you're willing, let's share with Phebe something about ourselves and what led us to sign up for that séance. It might be useful."

"Phebe, my name is Dana Pierce, I'm retired, and I've lived in Palm Springs for just over five years. I'm both a divorcee and a widow. My first two husbands, whom I married at an early age, were losers. Dan, the love of my life, passed away of cancer about a year before I moved here. Luckily, I've made good friends in the area and have found lots of interesting activities to pursue. Honestly, when Mallory told me about the séance, I thought, 'It's probably a big scam, but it gives me an excuse to see Idyllwild and escape the heat with my friends.'"

One by one, the others joined in. It turned out that Mallory and Dana had been close friends for several years, and although they didn't know much of her background, Emily had seamlessly joined them because of a shared interest in the arts. All three said they had attended the séance out of curiosity — not out of any particular need — though all were definitely séance skeptics.

"What about you, Phebe? What brought you to the séance?"

"I arrived in Palm Springs after escaping a failed long-term relationship. I needed to get away from Chicago and build a new life in a new place. I'm a bit embarrassed to admit it, but when I saw the poster advertising the séance, I thought, 'I might as well. I have nothing better to do. I'm trying to say yes to new experiences'."

"Where are you staying, Phebe?" asked Emily.

"For now, I'm staying at a Best Western downtown, but I need to find more permanent lodging so I can get these bags and boxes out of my car."

"I have an idea," interjected Mallory. "I have a small poolside casita that just became available. It's not fancy, but it's fully furnished and equipped with everything you'd need. If you're interested, you could drop by tomorrow afternoon to check it out. I'd love to have my next tenant be someone I know."

"What a generous offer," replied Phebe. "I'm definitely interested."

Emily steered the conversation back to the séance. "What were your impressions of the people who attended?" she asked.

"With the exception of that obnoxious Brad, they all

appeared to be nice and rather ordinary," said Dana. "As hard as it is for me to admit, aside from the sleaze factor, Brad is one deliciously sexy man." Dana closed her eyes, took a breath, then continued. "The quiet couple, Mr. and Mrs. Chen, seemed very sad. The young man said he had known their son. Did anyone catch his name?"

"I think he introduced himself as Lance," said Emily. "He said he was attending the séance to write an essay for a class assignment."

Emily went on. "What did you think of the older guy who was mourning his wife? I think his name was Arthur."

"He actually gave me his business card," Phebe responded, "though I think he's retired now. Evidently, he was an executive director of the Coachella Valley Library. He didn't strike me as the type of person who would attend a séance. It seems he's been grieving his wife's death for several months and may have reached out to the occult as a last desperate attempt to connect with her."

"You're right," said Dana. "He seemed to be in deep mourning."

"So," continued Emily, "who in the group seems most likely to be a murder victim?"

They explored theories without identifying anyone specifically. Brad Merrill was immensely unlikeable and an obvious choice as either the killer or a murder victim, but no one else present seemed a likely target or someone capable of murder. "Brad had just one goal for the evening," said Mallory, "to hook up with Annalore Dubois. Why would he want to murder any of the other participants?"

Emily spoke up. "You know, we've spent a lot of time talking about the others in the room, but what about us? Of course, we all have something in our past we would not willingly share. But have any of you been threatened or stalked lately? Aside from my abusive ex-husband, who is long gone, I can't think of anyone who would want to hurt me."

Dana's heart skipped a beat, and it took her a moment to catch her breath, because she harbored a horrible secret. No, she told herself, this was not something she was proud of or could share with anyone … ever. She said quickly, "Nope, can't think of anyone who would want to harm me. What about you, Mallory?"

Mallory thought for a moment. "No, my life is distinctly lacking in drama." She waited a moment and then spoke up again. "It's a reach, but I do have an issue with a former colleague from my New York days with Sam Stevens and she's a real piece of work. She shamelessly stole clients from me without a shred of remorse. I wouldn't trust her for a second. I haven't seen her for years and don't know if she's still involved with galleries and art museums or if she's even alive."

"Mmmm …," said Emily. "You're right. It does seem a stretch she could be involved clear across the continent after several years, but it's good to know you're concerned enough to mention her."

"Phebe? What about you?" Emily asked. "You mentioned a failed relationship."

Phebe closed her eyes and took a deep breath. "Trust me. My former partner has already moved on to his next conquest and seems perfectly happy. He's delighted I've left town and disappeared completely from his life."

"Here's a thought," offered Dana. "I'd like to consolidate everything we've discussed and do a bit of internet research on Annalore Dubois and all the séance participants. We definitely need more information before we can make any sense of all this. Tomorrow, before we leave, let's stop at Annalore's office and see if we can get a list of attendees. If she's there, maybe we can pump her for additional information. Later, I'll write up some notes and we can meet again in a couple of weeks to review them. Also, if any of you can think of anything I missed or should explore further, please send me a text."

"Great idea, Dana," they chorused. "Thanks for offering to do this."

The group visited for another half hour. Emily and Mallory, exhausted and needing sleep, took the bedroom and Phebe and Dana each took a big sofa bed in the living room.

The next morning, the group gathered in the inn's common area to share a delicious continental breakfast of fresh berries, orange juice, homemade vanilla scones and strong coffee. Mallory took the opportunity to issue an invitation.

"The Hanson Fine Art Gallery in Palm Springs is hosting a reception next Friday night, featuring the works of Rodin, Snowden and others. I can get invitations for all of us and it promises to be a very interesting evening. We can get dressed up, enjoy some fabulous wine and appetizers, and meet the Valley's most prestigious art representatives and collectors. Are any of you interested?"

"Absolutely!"

"Then it's a date," confirmed Mallory. "I'll be in touch with the details."

After breakfast, the group said good-bye to Phebe, who had an early appointment in Palm Desert.

Dana, Mallory and Emily walked over to the building where the séance had been scheduled the night before, expecting that the venue was also the site of Annalore Dubois' office. The outer door was locked when they arrived, and blinds were drawn. No signage appeared anywhere on the exterior of the building and no cars were parked outside. In short, it was as if the prior night's events had never occurred.

CHAPTER 4

The click, click, click of red-soled stilettos rang out as Tiffany Snow, art dealer extraordinaire and primary sales rep for Hanson Fine Art Gallery, headed toward the entrance. The tranquil notes of a harp greeted prospective buyers as they entered, leaving the gusting arid wind behind.

"Welcome! My name is Tiffany. I'm here for you and will be presenting artists throughout the gallery. Feel free to come to me at any time. You'll find your personalized name badges at the check-in kiosk to your right. Help yourselves to one of those glossy brochures. Champagne and hors d'oeuvres are available throughout the venue. Have fun!"

"Don't you just love her heels, Phebe? This is so exciting. Look here, it says: VIP guests may be invited by Hanson's to a private showing."

She tilted her head toward the check-in table where a

statuesque blonde dressed in a mauve St. John knit stood, her diamond earrings twinkling across the room. "I bet she'll be invited," Emily gushed. Unconsciously, she tightened her sapphire studs, the one heirloom from her great grandmother.

"Sure Emily, if she has clout or the bucks."

Phebe glanced to see who had caught Emily's attention. She saw the blonde and noticed that Dana and Mallory had checked in and were now helping themselves to caviar and glasses of champagne. And ...

Crap! I'd swear that's Toni Vitale standing there talking with Dana and Mallory. I should have known she'd find her way to California.

Phebe hadn't seen Toni in nearly a year. They'd met and shared mutual interests at A-list social events until Phebe dropped out. Her experience taught her Toni was cunning, a shark. She'd do anything to ensure she got the sale. You'd never guess it by her confident conversation and designer wardrobe.

Darn! Toni had spotted her, waved, and strolled over with Mallory and Dana in tow.

Mallory's eyebrows furrowed, and her lips pulled tight across her teeth. Dana looked worried, her usually smooth forehead wrinkled. Neither appeared to be pleased to be in Toni's company.

"Hello, Phebe darling. I haven't seen you since the LA opening. Great times we had." Her voice lowered, but not so low that others couldn't hear her say, "Oh, you poor dear. How are you holding up? I heard you got dumped. No doubt you have your own version of the story. Maybe you'll tell me sometime."

Same old bitch, Phebe thought as she remembered those days. She'd been enjoying the wine and hors d' oeuvres and was looking forward to a restful night in the casita she now rented from Mallory. "Oh, everything's just great, thanks." *It was until you showed up.*

"What a small world, seeing Mallory and now you. She tells me she knows you too. She and I were also colleagues in New York and often shared clients."

Toni's sharp eye caught sight of Emily's expensive sapphire studs. Taking her by the arm she led her to a half life-size bronze statue. Tiffany Snow could be heard saying "Thirty-eight of the original handmade sculpting tools of Auguste Rodin have survived him and been passed down through three generations of proteges."

Pointing to the statue, Toni whispered in Emily's ear, "Isn't it glorious? Such a rich history, and a bargain."

"It is impressive." *Toni is so beautiful and cultured. I'd love to be like her. Well, maybe not, after the way she just insulted Phebe.*

Feeling insecure and wanting a break from this unexpected pressure, Emily blurted, "I'm off to the ladies room."

Dana saw Toni smirk as Emily dashed off, and then saw her hugging a rough looking character with lamb-chop sideburns. The guy pulled what looked like a flask from his breast pocket and poured the liquid into a highball glass. *Where did he find that?*

Dana felt the hair rise at the nape of her neck and a chill run down her spine. *That woman is not to be trusted, and who's the guy?* She lifted another glass from the roving server and thought how uncomfortable Phebe seemed around Toni and how Toni was pushing Emily to buy that large statue. What in the world would she do with it? Paintings seem more Emily's style.

Phebe's voice brought Dana back from her thoughts. "Oh! Now that I'm comfortably housed, I thank you,

Mallory. I'd like all of us to get together at the casita to celebrate our friendship. How about Wednesday or Thursday?"

"Thanks, Phebe. I'm so happy you chose to take me up on the offer of the casita. I really am enjoying your company."

"Sounds like fun," said Dana while watching Toni put her arm through Emily's as soon as she exited the ladies' room and lead her further into the gallery. "I'll let Emily know as soon as Toni gets her hooks out of her. Also, I'm going to search the internet and hope to have information to share about those involved in the séance."

"Great! It's a date then."

Toni rejoined the group, accompanied by the muscular man now stroking his sideburns with the fingers of his right hand, while balancing what looked like scotch in his left. Evidently Emily had gotten away again.

"This is my dear friend and client, Forrest ... Forrest Williams. He has a painting he wants to sell – an original by Ecke, part of the Men Behind Gates series. Mallory, I told him of your expertise and that you'd be happy to appraise it for him for a nominal fee. I'll text you directions to his place."

"Nice meeting you, Mallory. Thanks for coming out to the ranch to appraise the painting for me. I've been told it's an unusual Ecke, but I know it's the real deal."

"Of course, it is," Toni cut in, then whispered into Forrest's ear and led him to a corner near the exit.

The evening was ending and though Mallory had chatted with many potential clients, Forrest Williams was the only real connection she'd made. He looked quite out of place in this elegant setting. Toni was nervy volunteering her, without asking, to appraise the painting. She'd gone as far as to state Mallory's willingness to check it out at his desert ranch.

Mallory had made no other connections. *I really must make some sales. This freelancing just isn't cutting it. My savings are nearly gone.*

Dana had agreed to meet her at the exit but Mallory was nowhere in sight.

The attendant gripped the door as a blast of wind whipped up Mallory's skirt. She could hear the palm trees groaning in the courtyard and was surprised to see the radiant light of day had turned inky black. Nothing was visible beyond the valet station. Guests, previously so lighthearted, were now scurrying to their cars, holding brochures over their heads as they dodged flying debris. She'd check inside one more time and then leave. Dana was a grown woman. Perhaps she'd found another way home.

CHAPTER 5

Dana preferred to ride rather than drive and Emily was willing to accommodate her.

Emily had been running the car's air conditioner against the afternoon heat, though it didn't muffle the noise of the looky-loos swarming through the area. Palm Springs and specifically, the Old Las Palmas neighborhood, was known for the annual mid-century modern tours that brought thousands of tourists from around the world.

Dana, a bit frazzled from watching Emily dodge the walking and cycling tourists, spotted a woman across the street from Mallory's home. She was standing on tiptoe, holding her camera high to get a shot over the breeze block wall into the private yard.

"Jeez, Emily. I wonder how she'd like it if someone did that in her neighborhood."

"Evidently, she couldn't get a good shot through the breeze block. We know that Modernism Week is only one of the many annual events Palm Springs is well known for, so we learn to smile and be inviting for a few weeks at a time. These homes and their history are remarkably interesting to many people, as most have wealthy owners today — even some Hollywood stars."

Pulling into Mallory's driveway, they noticed a discreet weathered bronze plaque affixed to the stone wall. It read:

The Harold & Lillian Crawford Residence
Designated Class 1 Historic Site

"I knew Mallory owned an historic home but didn't expect this. We've always met at public places like the coffee shop," said Emily as she pressed the intercom button.

"Hi. I see you made it," said Mallory. "Drive on through." The iron gate swung open with a creak then clanked shut once the car cleared the electric eye.

Mallory met them as they stepped out of the car. "Come on, let's go see what Phebe has done with the casita."

Walking along the south side of the L-shaped residence to the back of the property, they could smell the fragrant blossoms of orange, tangelo, and the prized ruby red grapefruit trees.

"Goodness Mallory, what a beautiful property! We saw the plaque on the wall. I knew you owned an historic home but had no idea it was registered as a Class I Historical Site. That must be quite a responsibility."

"Emily, that's a long story; really my parents' love story. They loved each other, Palm Springs, and this home. During WWII, Dad was an Army surgeon assigned to Torney General here in Palm Springs."

"I remember stories about the El Mirador Hotel, playground of the rich and famous, being converted to a military hospital."

"That's right, Emily. We know it today as Desert Regional Hospital.

"Dad loved the warm weather, after living in the bitter winters of North Dakota. My mother agreed, so after the war they became snowbirds for several years until 1965, when they came across this home. They packed up and moved to Palm Springs as permanent residents. The icing on the cake came thirty years later when they were approached by the Historical Society asking if they were interested in having their home registered on the Historic Site Registry. Mom and Dad were so pleased and worked hard to maintain the property according to the guidelines.

"Now it's mine, Emily. And I have to say, the upkeep and rules set out by the Historical Society make a tough nut to crack, expense-wise."

"I can imagine how difficult it must be to have to follow someone else's rules for your property," said Dana. "It really is a special place."

The three approached the casita, just as Phebe — drinks in hand — opened the door and stepped out.

"Welcome! I have everything set out, including your favorite Rombauer chardonnay, Dana."

"How thoughtful. I need to calm down after watching Emily navigate through all those people on the roads. It really was nerve-racking."

A shadow dashed in front of the fruit trees. "Oh my gosh! It's that woman who was taking pictures over the neighbor's wall. What the heck is she doing? Some nerve."

"I'll take care of this," sighed Mallory, approaching the woman. "How can I help you?"

Hanging her head, the woman mumbled, "I guess I got carried away with the history of these properties. Yours is beautiful. I stepped in after the car for just one quick picture and the gate closed behind me. The tour guide must be looking for me. He keeps counting everyone. I apologize and am so embarrassed. Can you please let me out?"

Without a word, Mallory entered the code to open the gate and the woman rushed out.

"Sorry ladies. That's never happened before. Phebe, let's get on with our party."

"Good idea. Be sure to try these crab balls from Costco," Phebe offered as they stepped out of the glaring sunlight and into the welcoming coolness of the casita. "They will really surprise you."

"Let me tell you about this casita," gushed Phebe. It's so spacious — about seven hundred square feet. There's the overstuffed sofa and two matching high-back chairs, all covered in this lovely quilted floral fabric. The main living space is separated from the sleeping area by this four-foot-tall glass block wall. The original olive-green appliances are perfect in this pink kitchen. Then there's the cozy bathroom, also pink to match the kitchen. I have my own private patio through the bedroom's French doors. I just love living here!"

"I see why you're so relaxed," commented Emily. "This is really a Shangri-La."

"I'm so happy here. I couldn't have found a better home and Mallory is the perfect friend and landlord. The paintings on the walls are from my own collection and have been in storage for nearly a year. It feels good to live with them again."

"I'm comfortable having you here, Phebe. My last tenant made me wonder if I wanted another."

Mallory sighed. "Now, thanks to Toni, I must drive out to some godforsaken date ranch near Joshua Tree that's probably off the grid. Anyone excited to join me? Remember, it may be a long desolate drive. How about you, Phebe?"

"Sure, I'll ride along."

"And Emily, we noticed how Toni glommed onto you at the gallery. Please be careful of her. She's not what she appears to be."

"I caught a glimpse of her real self when she so freely put Phebe down. I appreciate the warning, Mallory."

"There are more hors d'oeuvres on the glass table," Phebe informed them, as she juiced three freshly picked grapefruit and mixed up a batch of Greyhounds. "Please feel free to help yourselves while Dana fills us in on her internet discoveries."

"I've found a few interesting tidbits on social media regarding Annalore Dubois. Seems her earlier posts were under the name, Alex Dunbar. It looks like it's meant to be a secret, but Alex was searching for plastic and reconstructive doctors specializing in transgender surgeries."

"Oh my, Dana," exclaimed Mallory. "Wouldn't that put a damper on Don Juan Brad?"

"Yes, it certainly would!" Emily exclaimed as she settled down at one end of the sofa. "It's hard to imagine. She's so beautiful and feminine - the most feminine woman I've ever seen. Everyone is entitled to be who they are and thank goodness, that's possible nowadays."

"Do you think that had anything to do with her alarming pronouncement and the fact that she looked scared to death?"

"Maybe — maybe not, Mallory." Dana rose and poured herself half a glass of wine. "An old website explained that

Alex was raised in a haunted mansion in New Orleans. His mother claimed he was clairvoyant from childhood. Alex took clairvoyance a step further, becoming a medium in his early twenties, offering séances and claiming the spirits of recently deceased people communicated with him on a regular basis. Alex, now Annalore Dubois, is a most interesting person."

"Well, that's quite an eye-opener," Phebe chimed in. "Anything interesting about Brad or Arthur?"

"I couldn't find anything about Brad at all. All we know is what he willingly shared, if that's even true." Dana sighed. "He is handsome, though. I see why he has such a huge ego. Still, he's a bit much to take."

"I agree," said Phebe.

"Now Arthur Webster is a much different story," continued Dana. "The web search added to what he revealed about himself at the coffee shop. He seems to love books and really was the Executive Director of the Coachella Valley Library for twenty-five years."

"Yes, I believe I've heard of him," said Emily. He's highly educated and well-respected in the community. In fact, as we were dodging the crowd outside, there were two COPs — you know, Cops on Patrol. They were trying to keep all the tourists safely off the street. One looked just like Arthur. We waved and said hello, but I'm not sure he saw us."

"That's interesting," Dana said. "It could have been him, Emily. He's certainly civic-minded. Arthur seems to have always conducted himself with dignity. His life was what most people would consider boring, until as a grad student at Stanford, he met the gorgeous Martine Duval.

"The news articles describe her as a woman with large turquoise eyes, short, blond pixie hair, flawless skin, and a shapely body, who could simply walk into a room and all conversation would stop.

"That may seem a bit much for the bookish Arthur, but apparently, she was a French artist and highly intelligent as well."

Dana continued. "Arthur was quoted as saying when he married Martine, it was the best decision he'd ever made. The two enjoyed a long, loving marriage and raised two children —- adults now — who live on the east coast.

"When Martine died, her obituary was a tearjerker," Dana went on. "His perfect life seemed at an end. Later articles mentioned his early retirement and the fact that he was rarely seen in public. His children were quoted as saying they have little communication with him. It seems he became a recluse."

"Remember," said Mallory, "he told us when he saw a flyer advertising the séance, he was desperate, grasping at straws, and wondered if it could be possible to speak with Martine beyond the grave."

"I was amazed how much I found online, so I'm going to check out Toni and Forrest. They seem an odd pair. Also, I took the liberty of checking out what was on there about us."

Dana paused. "Mallory, it looks like your husband and Toni's had the same or similar names. Is that possible?"

"Oh, that's old news. I know she held a grudge against me for a while, but I doubt it has anything to do with this current situation."

The women were stunned by this latest information and Mallory's offhand dismissal of it. Why had she kept this a secret?

Rather than asking any more questions of Mallory, Dana opted to cover her surprise by refilling her wine glass and saying, "There's nothing about me on there, but I do understand how unsettled Arthur must feel. I have this recurring dream, a nightmare really. It scares the day-lights out of me."

"I'm so sorry to hear that, Dana. What's the nightmare about?" Phebe questioned.

"You know I ask for rides all the time. It's because I'm afraid the nightmare will come true."

"What's this nightmare about?" insisted Mallory.

"I'm driving down a dark mountain road. It's foggy and I can barely see. There's a sudden THUMP against the grill and I'm jolted into the dashboard. I've hit something hard. I'm so scared I hit a person."

"Oh my God!" Phebe exclaimed. "That is scary. No wonder you don't like to drive. But it's just a dream, Dana."

"Yes, it's just a dream. But it feels so real."

CHAPTER 6

"Oh! My! God!" Emily's excited shrieks could be heard from across the room, as the four women entered the Ooh-La-La Bistro. The place was ornate, with colorful walls, French Toulouse-Lautrec posters, lush green plants, the lilting voice of Edith Piaf filling the space, and lots of glittery touches in the lighting and decor.

"Shh! Emily. You'll get us all thrown out before we're even seated. Please! A little dignity," admonished Dana.

Emily giggled in response. "I can't help it, Dana. I can't believe all these gorgeous women are really men!" Mallory and Phebe chuckled at Emily's unexpected reaction to what was for her, a distinctly alien environment. Clearly, this was Emily's first visit to, what was reputed to be, Palm Springs' best drag brunch.

Earlier in the week, Phebe had seen a poster advertising the bistro, with its mouth-watering brunch menu and free-flowing champagne, its stunningly beautiful waitstaff, and — what promised to be — spectacular entertainment. What drew Phebe's attention was a photograph of the show's headliner; none other than the elusive medium, Annalore Dubois!

Texting her three friends, Phebe begged them to join her the following Sunday for some fun and an opportunity to find out more about the mysterious Ms. Dubois!

Approaching the check-in, Phebe gave her name and explained that she'd been promised a table for four near the stage, because she and her friends wanted to be up close and personal with the performers — especially Annalore.

The hostess, a striking blond with big hair, greeted them with a friendly smile. She wore a skin-tight leopard print sheath dress, red knee-high leather boots, and large silver hoop earrings.

"Unfortunately, our scheduled main performer is AWOL. No worries, though. The Coachella Valley is blessed with an abundance of talent, so it wasn't difficult to find a suitable replacement."

"What happened to Ms. Dubois?" asked Dana.

"We booked her act months ago and had been in touch with her until recently. She seemed eager to perform here. We've called her repeatedly to confirm and she seems to have disappeared! We'd hoped she would just show up. I can't imagine what's happened to her."

"When did you last hear from her?" asked Mallory.

"It's been a while, so we had to move on to Plan B. I know you're disappointed, but I guarantee you'll have a good time. If you'll follow me, I'll take you to your table, and make sure you get your first glass of bubbly!"

After the four were settled and their champagne poured, Mallory offered a toast. "Here's to the memorable

Annalore Dubois, wherever she is. To her good health!"
Everyone raised their glasses and took a long sip.

Dana remarked, "Well, this whole thing about Annalore
Dubois is weird! I wish we could find a way to connect
with her. I can't believe she would blow off a paying gig."

"Yeah," answered Phebe. "Everything about that evening in Idyllwild was strange."

Emily added, "Even though I'm super disappointed
that we can't see Annalore, I'm excited to have our brunch
and see the show. Everyone says it's spectacular!"

While the women looked at their menus, Dana excused
herself to go to the restroom. As one might expect, the
ladies' room was very elegant, with a mural of a Parisian
bordello filling one wall. There were crisp white tiled
floors, green ferns and philodendrons arranged artfully,
jewel-encrusted mirrors, and gold fixtures on the sinks.
The scene was enhanced with the faint aroma of a flowery
cologne.

After doing her business, and before refreshing her
makeup, Dana took a moment to chug down a mouthful
of vodka from a small silver flask that nestled discreetly
in her purse. As the familiar sensation of warmth surged
through her body, she worried that her friends might soon
catch on to her increasing fondness for liquor.

*What am I going to do? Booze is the only way I can forget my
guilt-ridden nightmares!*

Shoving the tiny flask deep into her purse, a distracted Dana exited the restroom and suddenly found herself
chest to chest with a tall man walking away from the hostess station.

"Oh! Excuse me! I'm so sorry," Dana exclaimed, stepping back. "I didn't see you there."

She looked up and saw a familiar face smiling back at

her. Oh no! It was the devastatingly handsome, but obnoxious, guy from the séance — Brad something. But he looked different today. The man she remembered had presented himself as the worst kind of American tourist, wearing baggy shorts, a loud Hawaiian shirt, flip-flops and a baseball cap. Today he looked as if he'd stepped out of the cover of *GQ* magazine!

Dana blushed as Brad's laser-like charcoal eyes focused directly on hers, seeming to pierce her innermost soul.

Does this guy ever blink? Dana squirmed.

"We've met before," Brad said. "You were in Idyllwild last month at the séance."

"I was," replied Dana. "And you were the eager fellow pursuing the medium."

"Guilty!" Brad responded, maintaining eye contact.

"Then you're going to be very disappointed today. Annalore Dubois won't be performing.

"I'm aware."

"And yet, here you are."

This guy can't possibly be gay, Dana thought. *And yet … he could be … maybe bisexual. Or not. That would be a pity for straight women everywhere! Mmm…*

Dana paused for a moment to appraise this new, more attractive Brad. He was one of those uber-sexy, African-American men, who exuded confidence from every pore. An older version of Regé-Jean Page from the Netflix series, "Bridgerton," he also bore a slight resemblance to the actor, Idris Elba. Sporting a kind of modern badass look, Brad's clothes fit his chiseled body like a glove. With a diamond stud in his left ear and his hair cropped short, he dressed simply, but expensively in jeans, a gray polo shirt, and a fabulous black leather jacket. The outfit was topped off with Adidas' sporty Stan

Smith casual shoes and Ray-Ban Wayfarer sunglasses.

Hubba-hubba! thought Dana, obviously impressed, but wary.

"I'm Brad Merrill. And you are …?"

"Dana Pierce. What are you doing here?"

"One might ask you the same thing, Ms. Pierce," replied Brad with a twinkle in his eye.

"I'm here with my friends from the séance. You met them … Phebe, Mallory and Emily. We heard the drag brunch was a real hoot and, of course, we were curious about Annalore Dubois."

"Please come join me at my table, Dana, and we can get better acquainted."

Dana's heart started to pound and she felt breathless. *Oh God! I want to know more but he's revealing nothing about himself. He's really enjoying this.*

"Uh no," she hesitated. "I'd better get back to my friends."

"Then you won't mind if I follow you to your table and say hello. As I recall, your friends were quite a lively group!"

"It's a free country," said Dana. "I'm sure they'll remember you from Idyllwild."

In no time at all, Brad had completely charmed the ladies, and they had invited him to join them. Pretty soon they were all chatting amiably and ordering another bottle of champagne.

"Brad," said Emily. "You seem different today from how you were at the séance."

"Really? How so?" Brad responded.

"Emily!" Dana interjected. "This isn't the time or the place. Just let it go. Please!"

"To the contrary, Dana. I want to hear more," challenged

Brad with a grin. "Please continue, Emily."

"Well …" Emily went on, trying to be tactful. "I don't mean to offend, but before, you seemed a bit on the bossy side, arrogant. Maybe even sexist."

"I see," said Brad comfortably. "Is there anything else?"

"Mmm, that about covers it. But today, you seem like a different person."

Mallory spoke up, "Which makes me wonder, what was the real reason you went to the séance? I don't buy for a minute that you went only to hit on Ms. Dubois. I think something else was going on."

"How do you know I wasn't on a secret mission?" Brad joked.

"Yeah, right," scoffed Phebe. "Obviously, you're a spy."

"I was at the séance on a simple fact-finding adventure. If I said any more about it, I'd have to kill you," Brad responded, laughing.

Dana abruptly changed the subject and the group moved on to other, safer topics.

Eventually, brunch orders were given and more champagne consumed. As advertised, the entertainment that followed was lavish. There were musical performances, dazzling dance numbers, over-the-top costumes and comedic skits.

Later that afternoon, the thoroughly satisfied — and slightly tipsy — foursome said good-bye to Brad and thanked him for buying two extra bottles of champagne. As they were leaving, Brad pulled Dana aside.

"You can't get away that easily, Ms. Pierce. I've got my eyes on you."

He slipped a business card into her hand and added, "I'm new to this area and need a tour guide to the local attractions. Call me and we'll meet for coffee."

With that, Brad winked, turned around and walked away.

After she got home, Dana could think of nothing but Brad Merrill. At the drag brunch, she had seen him with fresh eyes and realized his personality was strikingly different from the way he'd appeared at the séance. And he was so handsome. She had immediately taken notice of his smooth-shaven, coffee-colored skin and dark brown eyes that seemed to be in constant search for something or someone. Everything was different about him.

Brad had been friendly, respectful and kind — a far cry from the loud, misogynistic oaf from the séance. *It might be nice to get to know him*, she thought, surprising herself.

Dana poured herself a glass of wine, sat on the lounge in her patio and continued to replay the afternoon in her mind. For the first time in months, she'd forgotten her troubles and enjoyed having fun with her friends. The unexpected arrival of Brad had only added to her pleasure.

Her thoughts were interrupted by the ringing of her cell phone.

"Hello?"

"Dana, it's Brad Merrill."

"My goodness," she blurted. "I didn't expect to hear from you. How did you get my number?" Her heart started to pound.

"I'm a spy. Remember? I can find out anything," he joked. "Listen, Dana, after the séance and the drag brunch, I was afraid we'd gotten off on the wrong foot. I'd like to start over and get to know you. Would you like to go out for coffee later this week? I particularly like the coffee at Koffi on Tahquitz Canyon. Do you know it?" Brad hoped she would say yes. "If you're uncomfortable with me picking you up, I'll be happy to meet you there."

Dana was so surprised, she had trouble breathing. Was Brad asking her out on a date? She didn't know what to say.

Brad continued. "I understand that you probably have a lot of questions about me, and I'll willingly answer them. I'll want to know your story too. What brought you to the séance and the brunch? How do you know the other three women? You all seem so nice — very intelligent, good conversationalists." Brad was adding adjective after adjective.

"Brad, you don't need to keep piling it on. I get the picture," Dana finally laughed. "I'd love to meet you for coffee."

When Dana told her friends about her coffee date with Brad, they were more than happy Dana had accepted his invitation. She had been in such a bad place recently, they hoped this flirtation would lift her spirits.

CHAPTER 7

One afternoon, a few days later, Dana arrived at Koffi before Brad and sat in her car waiting for him. *My God, he's gorgeous,* she thought, as Brad walked over and opened her car door. Dana slid out, took his hand, and thanked him.

It couldn't have been a more perfect winter day in Palm Springs. The skies were clear and sunny, the air was a balmy 70 degrees, and it seemed that flowers were in bloom everywhere. After getting their drinks inside, Dana and Brad chose a lovely outdoor table that offered a magnificent view of the mountains along with enough privacy for intimate conversation.

Dana wasn't certain what to say. She thought it would be best to let Brad start, and he was ready to do just that.

"Dana, I work for a government agency and I'm here on temporary assignment. My work is sometimes dangerous and requires me to work undercover. That's what was going on at the séance in Idyllwild. And that is precisely why you were so put off by my behavior. I wish I could tell you more, but right now, I'm unable to do so."

"So, you really are a spy," said Dana. "Not the obnoxious, egocentric, handsome man you portrayed," she smiled mischievously. "Actually, we've all been wondering what was really going on with you and the mysterious medium that night. Were any of us in danger?"

"Well, I am handsome, don't you think? But I would never call myself a spy. Most of the time I'm just a boring, but dedicated, civil servant. Maybe I'll write my memoirs one day and reveal all my secrets."

"I certainly hope so."

The ice was broken and the two began a non-stop conversation. For the first time in months, Dana felt energized and the smile on her face wasn't forced. Brad was equally animated. They discovered they shared many interests, and both had a dry, witty sense of humor.

After years of meaningless relationships with lots of women, Brad felt something new in his gut. Dana was special and he was hooked.

Hours went by, and the two could've continued talking into the evening. Finally, Dana said she needed to get going.

"Understood," agreed Brad. "This has been wonderful. May I take you out to dinner sometime soon?"

"I'd like that, Brad. You can even call for me at my condo. I'm in South Palm Springs, not hard to find." Dana gave Brad her home and email addresses.

"I'll be in touch soon," he promised.

"Great!"

The two got up from their table. When Brad's arm lightly touched her back, Dana felt a frisson of electricity through her body.

Wow, Dana! When have you felt like this before?

Dana pressed a button on her key fob, unlocking her car door. Brad opened it for her and hesitantly put his arms around her for a parting hug. Before turning around to go, Brad kissed her lightly on the cheek.

"I'll see you soon, Dana." He had so much more to tell her.

That night, Dana slept soundly without nightmares and awoke fresh and happy. Since the death of her husband, Dana had met no one who interested her, and now Brad was in her life. *Maybe, sometime, I can tell him about my accident. I have to tell someone. I know that's why I've been drinking so much. I need to get control of that.*

CHAPTER 8

Where are we going?" Phebe asked from the passenger's seat, as she stared at the desolate landscape. She looked down, confused, at the map resting on her jeans-clad lap.

"We've just passed the turn-off for Pioneer Town," replied Mallory. "Believe it or not, Paul McCartney once performed there."

"I don't believe it! We've also passed Old Woman Springs Road. Do you think it was named after an old woman who couldn't remember her name?"

"I wouldn't be surprised," chuckled Mallory. "That road is a short-cut from here to I-15, the interstate that goes to Vegas."

"I've been researching the high desert," said Phebe. "Did you know that U2 made this area famous in the '80s? There's also something called an 'Integraton,' built by George Van Tassel, who was a wacky ufologist. He claimed the Integraton was capable of rejuvenation, anti-gravity, and time travel. Makes me wonder what else may exist in the high desert. Slow down, Mallory! We're coming to the turn-off."

Mallory gently tapped the brakes and turned her yellow Lamborghini — her precious "Monet" — onto what appeared to be a dirt road. Phebe smiled, suddenly noticing that Mallory matched her car. She was colorfully attired in dark yellow pants and a silk blouse in a yellow floral print.

"This doesn't look much like a road, but there's that single Joshua tree bent over nearly touching the large rock that we were told to look for."

"Will your car be all right?"

"Monet is amazing!" Mallory exclaimed as she swerved to miss a giant rock by the side of the road.

As Monet gracefully climbed up the slope, Phebe spotted other landmarks that were drawn on the map Toni had supplied. Unfortunately, she still saw no sign of a house. The view ahead revealed nothing but arid land with giant rocks and Joshua trees.

"Tell me more about this man we're going to see and the piece of art he wants to sell."

"We know his name is Forrest Williams from the gallery opening and Toni says he has a great art collection. That's about all I know."

"I guess we'll find out more today," Phebe said as she gazed at two enormous boulders, side by side, at the end of the road. "Mallory, slow down! It looks like we're not going to get any further."

Mallory stopped the car while Phebe hopped out to approach the two big rocks. Phebe realized there was sufficient space for a car to get through and saw tire tracks showing others had been there, so she waved Mallory forward.

Mallory pulled ahead and navigated Monet carefully between the boulders, with Phebe kicking up dust as she followed on foot. What greeted them on the other side of the rocks was a descent into a valley lush with date palms, hiding low-slung buildings.

"Where the hell are we?" wondered Phebe.

Mallory shrugged her shoulders. "Hop in. We're about to find out." She nudged Monet down the hill into an oasis-like valley, where they found themselves surrounded by well-tended date palms that lined the road. Further along, they spied a large greenhouse.

"Probably growing marijuana," Phebe whispered. Mallory grinned in agreement.

"Where are we? This is the middle of nowhere." Looking at each other, they broke into nervous giggles.

Pulling up in front of an imposing residence, they looked at each other for moral support and got out of the car.

At that moment, Toni burst out of the front door, waving her ever-present purple scarf that matched her slacks and blouse.

"Welcome! Welcome! Come inside and say hi to Forrest."

After one last glance around, Mallory and Phebe followed Toni into a small dark vestibule.

Passing through, the women noticed an ornate dagger hanging on the wall. Phebe grasped Mallory's hand and squeezed it hard.

"Have they finally arrived?" growled an irritated male voice coming from another room.

"Yes, they're here" replied Toni.

Toni led the two into a large room, whose plain walls were hung with paintings. The room was a windowless gallery with a large round table in the middle, surrounded by comfortable revolving chairs. The table held what looked like, individual lighting for each painting.

"Mallory and Phebe, you remember Forrest Williams from the Hanson Gallery opening," said Toni.

The women smiled as they greeted Forrest, remembering the 5'11", brown-eyed, self-styled silver fox, who sported scraggly facial hair. The two snuck an amused look at each other, wiggled their eyebrows and wondered to themselves if Forrest knew he was wearing his pajamas.

"Follow me. Let's have something to drink before we do business."

Phebe smiled and dumped her photography equipment by one of the revolving chairs.

Forrest led the women into a pleasant dining room with floor to ceiling windows, offering a majestic view that extended to the other end of the valley. Once there, he said, "Excuse me for a moment. I'm going to the kitchen to help Maria bring in our refreshments."

While they waited for Forrest, the three women sat down at a table facing the windows where they could admire the view. They noticed more date groves and oddly enough, a group of what looked like white palm trees. Phebe wondered out loud what they were. Toni explained they were quite rare, didn't bear fruit and were only sold for elegant landscaping projects. She went on to tell Phebe and Mallory that no one really knew how Forrest found this place or much about who he really was.

Toni then launched into a detailed description of the date ranch's elaborate water system, which originated from underground hot springs. For irrigation purposes, the water had to be cooled.

"Yes, and it's a big nuisance!" Forrest interrupted,

entering the dining room, followed by a woman carrying a big tray of cookies and beverages. She placed the tray on the table.

"What would you like to drink?" asked Forrest. We have tea, coffee, and water. Maria also baked some snickerdoodles, and they're still warm from the oven."

They each requested coffee and continued to discuss the magnificent view. While Mallory asked more questions of Toni and Forrest about the date groves and the irrigation system, Maria poured their coffee and handed out plates and napkins. At one point, Mallory quickly nudged Phebe and gestured at a nearby painting, signaling silently that Phebe should take a photo of it. Phebe took out her iPhone and shot several photos while Mallory continued to distract Toni and Forrest with conversation.

"Why do you have your phone out?" snapped Forrest, startling Phebe.

Phebe smiled and explained that she was just checking for messages. Forrest scowled and passed around the plate of snickerdoodles. The group made small talk as they drank their coffee and munched on the tasty cookies. As they were about to return to the gallery, Forrest's phone rang and he excused himself.

Moving on to the gallery, the ladies waited patiently, but couldn't help overhearing parts of the conversation, since Forrest had raised his voice.

"No! I'm not going to bail you out again. What yellow Lamborghini are you talking about? Are you kidding me? I'm done!" he shouted and abruptly ended the call.

Startled, Phebe and Mallory looked at one another. Why was someone talking about Monet?

Forrest entered the gallery and joined the women at the

table. He flipped a switch to turn on a spotlight focused on one painting — the Ecke.

"This is the Ecke I want to sell."

"Phebe, will you please take photos? Do an assortment of close-up and distance shots," instructed Mallory. Turning she asked, "Forrest, do you have the provenance for this piece?"

"Of course he does," hissed Toni. "Why would you ask such a thing?"

"Toni, you know I have to ask for documents."

Toni opened a drawer in the table and removed a file. "Here you are," she said, handing it to Mallory. "Do you need anything else?"

"No problem. I'll have everything I need as soon as Phebe finishes up with the photos."

As they were leaving, Mallory extended her hand to Forrest. "It's been a pleasure. I'll get back to Toni in a couple of days to let her know what I've come up with. Does that work for you and Toni?"

They both nodded.

"Then Phebe and I are off. Thank you for the coffee and cookies."

Back in the comfort of their car, the ladies sat for a moment, shaking their heads, still wondering who Forrest Williams really was and why he had a ranch in this god-forsaken place.

"Quick, let's get out of here," said Mallory, firing up Monet's engine. She sped up and out of the valley, slowing down to navigate carefully between the two guardian rocks.

Back on the road heading home, Phebe asked Mallory why she wanted photos of the painting in the dining area.

Mallory explained that it was a piece she could sell at once to a buyer she knew.

"I was excited as soon as I saw that dagger in the vestibule when we arrived. I had a hunch there would be more valuable works of art there and I couldn't wait to feast my eyes on them!"

Phebe then asked about the other piece in the gallery — the Ecke Forrest wanted her to appraise. Mallory threw her head back, laughing.

"It's a fake."

CHAPTER 9

The drive back to Palm Springs seemed to take forever, even though the two friends spent the time recapping their visit.

"That does it," chuckled Phebe. "I'm convinced the guy is a Nazi war criminal who's gone rogue and built himself a fortress in a place no one would ever visit. He probably has a hidden brigade of blond-haired, blue-eyed Hitler youth cultivating his date ranch. I can just picture them goose-stepping through the palm groves."

"I'd agree with you if his age matched up with the war years," snickered Mallory. "He looks to be in his late 50s, which would mean he was born well after the end of World War II."

"Just the same, our friend Forrest is clearly a strange duck. Could you believe he was wearing pajamas? I'd love to know who was on the other end of that call, since it sounded like it was about Monet."

"Yeah. That was a scary development. There's no question Forrest is eccentric; maybe even dangerous. Like you, I have a ton of questions," said Mallory.

"Well let's put those questions in writing before we forget them," countered Phebe, pulling out a notebook and pen from her purse.

"Mallory, my first question is, how did you know so quickly that his Men Behind Gates is a fake?"

"Forrest answered that question himself at the Hanson Gallery. Remember? He said a friend had questioned the work's authenticity because it lacked the heavy textures typical of Ecke. When I saw the painting, I knew at once it was an exceptional forgery. More important, Toni would've known it too and, because she's so familiar with my skills, she would have known I would not authenticate a forgery. I can't imagine why she would want me to be part of this ridiculous scheme. I just know there's something else going on with her."

"Well," interjected Phebe, "given those circumstances, why didn't you tell Forrest right away that the painting was a fake?"

"Honestly, because the situation was so disturbing and unpredictable, I wanted to put some distance between us and the Forrest/Toni duo. I remember her shady deals in New York and I'm sure you do, too. I'd prefer Toni not be present when I tell Forrest."

"That's probably a good call, Mallory, since we both know her history. Let's just get our questions written down and we can address them one by one when we get home."

Mallory agreed and the two began listing their questions. They were:

• Who is Forrest Williams and what is his real relationship with Toni?

• The painting was a fake. Why did Toni think Mallory would go along with providing a fraudulent appraisal?

• Who called Forrest about the Lamborghini and what did he or she want?

• What's the best way for Mallory to tell Forrest the Ecke isn't authentic?

• What's the real story of Forrest's extensive art collection?

It was late in the afternoon when Mallory and Phebe finally arrived home. The sun had just dipped beyond the mountains and the air had cooled. The citrus blossoms wafted their sweet fragrance as the two tired travelers sat on adjoining lounges by the pool enjoying glasses of a Chateau Montelena chardonnay.

Mallory spoke up first. "I have an idea, Phebe. Excuse me while I call Dana.

"Dana? This is Mallory. Phebe and I just got back from a very strange visit to Forrest Williams' compound out beyond Joshua Tree." She paused while Dana responded.

"Oh, yes. That's a long story in itself, to be told another day when there's more time. Look, I need your research skills, if you're willing. I'd like you to do a deep dive on Forrest Williams. Find out everything you can about him — his history, his business and personal life, where he's lived and traveled, any crimes or prison time served. You get the idea. Are you up for it?" She paused. "Great! How soon can you get back to me? Really? Thanks so much."

"She's in," announced Mallory. "Our Dana does excellent research and is happy to help us. She'll start tonight and will let us know immediately when she has some answers."

"Great!" said Phebe, pouring herself another glass of

chardonnay. "Are you ready to talk about what you'll say in your phone call to Forrest?"

Mallory nodded and the two began discussing options for giving Forrest the bad news. Luckily, they had time to work out the conversation. Mallory took a deep breath and said, "As far as I'm concerned, there's only one way to do it. Tell him the truth."

At that moment Mallory's phone rang and she could tell from the caller ID that it was Forrest. Mallory closed her eyes and counted to ten before answering.

"Hello, Forrest."

Forrest wasted no time. "I need answers fast," he practically shouted. "Toni said you were the best in the business, so I know you have results for me now."

"What's the big hurry, Forrest?"

"I already have a buyer for the Ecke, and he's promised big bucks for it, once it's authenticated."

"Forrest, I'm sorry, but that won't be possible. Your Ecke is a fake — a very good fake, but nonetheless a forgery."

"C'mon. That wasn't the answer I was expecting. Tell me why you think it's a forgery."

"Any expert would notice immediately that the issues are with the brush strokes, the layering, texture and the colors used."

"Bullshit! You're lying, bitch! Here's what I want you to do. Get back in your car right now and get your ass up here and show me in person why you're so sure the Ecke is a fake."

"Excuse me?" Mallory responded in a strong, calm voice. "There's no need to be rude. Forrest, I'm willing to explain my appraisal in person at my convenience, and I'll use that opportunity to collect my fee from you."

Forrest, though outraged, was clearly desperate to have Mallory return to his date ranch as soon as possible. He stopped himself from telling her he only intended to pay her if she authenticated the Ecke. Instead, he paused for a moment and then continued in a softer, more pleasing tone.

"Understood. Can you come out tomorrow evening?"

"No. I'd prefer driving out in the morning, probably with a friend. I won't be able to stay long, but we can get our business done. I have a luncheon appointment with my neighbor, who's working with the Palm Springs Police Department. I can be at your place at 10:30."

"If that's what you want. You're aware your friend Toni is convinced the Ecke is the real thing."

"I doubt it," replied Mallory. "In any case, we can clear everything up in the morning. Good night."

After Mallory and Forrest concluded their phone call, the two women remarked on Forrest's unexpected rage and his demeaning language. Mallory was comfortable with her lie about meeting for lunch with a police officer. At least it would give her a good excuse to end the meeting and should keep her safe.

After a brief discussion, the two women ordered Thai food from GrubHub, enjoyed dining in Mallory's outdoor kitchen, and finally said good night.

Exhausted, Mallory climbed the back stairs, entering through the kitchen, and headed straight to her bedroom. She turned on the bedside lamp, kicked off her sandals, plopped down in the cozy boudoir chair next to her bed and closed her eyes. Just as she began to drift off to sleep, the phone rang, interrupting her solitude.

Enough already! She had no intention of continuing

the disturbing discussion with Forrest tonight.

"Hello," Mallory answered sharply.

"It's Toni. There's something I want to ask you before you share your results with Forrest."

"Yes?"

"Well, is the Ecke real or not?"

"You know the answer to that as well as I do, Toni. Of course it's a forgery."

"But that's not what you're going to tell Forrest."

"What do you mean?"

"Your final documents to Forrest will authenticate, without question, that the Ecke is exactly what he expects it to be."

"No Toni, it won't. I've built my reputation very carefully over the years and my personal integrity is everything. I won't lie."

"If you don't, I will destroy you. I have international connections in the art world you can't even imagine. Just a few words to the right people and your career is 'toast.' I've been following your activities for the past couple of years and I know you're almost broke."

Mallory paused and took a deep breath before speaking.

"I never respond to threats, Toni. My ethics are the basis of my reputation. By the way, I've already told Forrest I can't authenticate the Ecke. As far as I'm concerned, this conversation is over. Don't bother me again."

And with that, Mallory ended the call, turned out the lights and fell into a restless sleep.

CHAPTER 10

Later that night: home of Toni Vitale

W ho the hell's calling me at this time of night?" grumbled Toni, not willing to admit she had been guilty of the same indiscretion just a couple of hours earlier.

She was irritated, not knowing exactly how she was going to deal with Mallory after her refusal to authenticate Forrest's painting.

Pulling on her shoes as she sat on the edge of her custom-made cherrywood sleigh bed, she reached across to the nightstand to silence her cell phone. The familiar "nah nah nah nah" from the Twilight Zone's distinctive theme alerted her to the caller's identity.

Toni loved her bedroom furniture and didn't mind admiring it at four in the morning. However, she worried her comfortable life was in jeopardy. All because of one idiot.

Irritated, she said "Why the fuck are you calling me at this hour?"

"What did you say?" the voice replied menacingly.

Listening to the caller, she thought, *This is ridiculous!*

"Screw you!" she said, slamming the phone down. At this time of night, she didn't want to talk to anyone — least of all, Forrest.

"You deserve to burn, Forrest!" she cursed.

Just as she had taken a slow deep breath, the phone went off again. *What the hell! I really must change that annoying ring tone.*

Grabbing the phone, she shrieked, "What do you want? Do you know what time it is, asshole? Call me at a civil hour. Then we can talk."

"Of course, I know it's late. I can't sleep. Don't hang up," commanded Forrest in his deep gravelly voice — a voice she once yearned to hear. "We need to talk now!"

Pressing the off button, Toni hoped he would get the message and not call back. She needed to call Mallory and prepare for her visit.

The ominous tone again brought the phone to life. "Oh my God!"

Taking a deep breath, Toni shrugged and answered. "Okay, you win, but make it quick. This call won't be pretty, I can guarantee that!"

"What I have to say isn't pretty either!" Forrest responded. "How did Mallory find out the painting was a fake?"

"What are you talking about? How do you know she thinks it's a fake?" Toni asked. "I haven't talked to Mallory since we were together at the ranch. Who else knew?"

Forrest's response was a heavy sigh.

Realizing he wasn't giving up, Toni pulled on a lavender

cashmere sweater and headed down the hall toward the kitchen. *I need a jolt!*

"Forrest, I have no idea how she found out, but it certainly wasn't from me. Please explain why I would tell her it's a fake! Remember, she is a professional. She evidently doesn't need money as badly as we anticipated. And why the hell are you calling me at this hour?"

There was no response from Forrest.

"Are you still there, Forrest?" His grunt informed her that he was. Toni pressed the espresso button on her Miele upscale bean-to-brew coffee system, the one she had pilfered when she left the New York gallery. A malicious grin crossed her lips. This machine was a bit large for one person, but she wasn't sorry she'd taken it.

Tossing her phone not so quietly on the granite counter, she reached into the cupboard and pulled out her purple Murano glass coffee cup, her favorite — the one she'd bought in Italy. She could hear Forrest's berating voice echoing off the hard granite.

"Sounds like you're threatening me, Forrest," she hollered at the phone. "What on earth for?"

The warm inviting aroma of coffee filled the room. After taking the first sip, she smiled. She could now see a vague light at the end of this tunnel.

"Maybe Bud told her. What a mistake. You tell him too much and what he isn't told he overhears. It seems to me he was unhappy when you told him no Lamborghini. Maybe he decided to blow you off!"

Forrest's voice rose. "Toni, don't give me any shit. You know how deep you are into this. How do you think you'd look in an orange jumpsuit?"

"You don't want to threaten me, Forrest. We've had a good run with Pascal since Iraq; just a few more sales and we can really be finished. However, if push comes to shove who do you think the authorities will believe … you or me?"

The phone went dead.

Really …

Glad the call was over, she turned her attention to the Miele and gently pressing the touchscreen, she opted for a double espresso. She'd need the caffeine to get everything ready for Mallory. Holding the warm cup in her hands, she hurried to her home office. An electronic eye lit the room as she approached.

A large painting of purple lilacs hung on the wall behind her chair. Setting the coffee on the desk, she removed the painting, revealing a safe. After another admiring glance at the lilacs, Toni carefully leaned the painting against the wall.

She knew the digital code by heart; after all, it was her wedding date. A soft musical tone confirmed the safe was now open. Pulling out a stack of unmarked files, she turned to place them on the corner of the desk and heard a thud as something heavy fell to the floor.

Leaning over, she saw it wasn't the paperweight, but her gold-plated Tariq, the pistol she'd brought back from Iraq. Picking up the gun, she tenderly rubbed her thumb across the medieval warrior emblem, then bringing the gun to eye level, she stretched out her arm and took aim. Just for a moment.

Comforted, Toni placed the gun in the center drawer on the right-hand side of the desk.

Settled into her desk chair, she reached for her cup, enjoying the last sips of the strong brew. There, at the edge of the desk, sat the oversized paperweight embedded with flowers, a nod to her femininity.

Toni began methodically going through the files and soon found the one she was looking for. Clearing the desk, she opened the file. Yes, everything was there. She laid the documents out on the desk, a few at a time, and snapped pictures with her phone, then gathered the pages and took them across the room to the printer, set the number icon to 4 and copied each page.

When the printer stopped, she returned the pages to her desk, laying copies of the first page out four times. Then the second page and the third, until all the pages had been placed into the four piles.

Pleased with herself, Toni folded the papers and placed each packet into individual Priority envelopes.

Pulling out the top drawer, she retrieved her old address book — the book where she kept her most important addresses. Old school for sure, but no internet exposure.

Toni wrote a different address on each envelope and ran them through her postage machine.

Nearly finished, she sighed, placed the stamped envelopes in the drawer on top of the gun, retrieved a key from the safe and locked the drawer.

Satisfied, she put the key back in the safe and gently returned the lilacs to their place on the wall, hiding the safe. Now, all she had to do was get Mallory over here and show her who was really in charge. She smirked, knowing how scared Mallory would be.

She raised her cup in a toast to herself. "We'll see who wins! Mallory, Forrest, Pascal — I'm coming for you!"

CHAPTER 11

Awakened from a fitful sleep, Mallory sat curled up in one of the damask upholstered chairs Vincenzo had given her for her last birthday, the last birthday they'd spent together, the last day he was alive. The chairs sat in an alcove in their bedroom. The two had enjoyed sitting there and talking about the day's activities. Tears streamed down her cheeks.

Oh Ceni, why did you have to die so young? We had so many plans.

Mallory caressed the chair's pillow, holding it as tightly as possible. It reminded her so much of the vibrancy of his life, strong and protective. The muted red flowers in the fabric swam before her eyes. *I don't know what to do. I'm going to have to sell this property and lose my parents' beloved legacy. I have no job and when your trust passed to your relatives after your death, I was left with no income. Having Phebe here does help.*

Mallory grabbed a tissue from a decorative box on the

table next to her, wiped her eyes and began speaking to herself again. *Mallory, pull yourself together. You're a survivor. Remember that. You are a survivor.*

When Mallory and Toni worked at the same gallery in New York, Toni went on vacation to Italy and returned with a husband, Vincenzo Vitale. It was a marriage created in haste. Toni and her new husband couldn't say a civil word to each other. The growing friction between the two was palpable. Toni left the firm without telling Mallory, and went to the House of Hamid. Toni wanted to go to the Middle East to bring back high-priced carpets and rugs, and this firm would get her there. At least that was her plan.

Vincenzo remained in New York and rented another apartment in Manhattan. Months after the divorce was final, he stopped at a neighborhood bar for a glass of wine, and spotted Mallory sitting alone at a table, looking beautiful and approachable. Since the place was crowded, she invited him to join her. They became inseparable after that evening, and by Christmas were married and living in Palm Springs.

When Ceni had his fatal heart attack, they had been happily married for almost sixteen years. Ceni had taken over the management of Mallory's family estate and made himself responsible for paying all the bills and upkeep. It was the happiest time in Mallory's life. She adored her husband and couldn't have been more grateful for his help in keeping the Crawford legacy alive.

Her soliloquy was interrupted by the loud ringing of her cell phone.

"Hello." Mallory answered in a sleepy voice.

Toni's angry voice greeted her on the other side.

"Mallory, this is Toni. We need to talk. Stop whatever you're doing right now and get your ass over to my house!"

"No way! I'm about to crawl into bed."

"That can wait. I need to see you. Trust me, you don't want to suffer the consequences of not meeting. I guarantee it will be worth your time."

"Toni, I'm very tired. Can't we do this tomorrow morning over a cup of coffee?"

"No, it has to be now." Toni was insistent.

Mallory was afraid Toni would try to do something illegal. She knew Toni had lost a very lucrative job in New York because of her unethical practices. She had no desire to renew her relationship with Toni. Until the Hanson Gallery event in Palm Springs, they hadn't seen each other since before Toni's divorce. Mallory wondered what had brought Toni to this part of the country.

Against her better judgment, Mallory acquiesced.

"All right if you insist, Toni. But I don't know where you live."

"In Old Las Palmas, just beneath the mountain. It's the new midcentury modern; dark gray, white trim, double-sized wood and glass door, painted bright purple. You can't miss it."

"It'll take me a few minutes."

"I'll be waiting."

CHAPTER 12

Frustrated, Mallory threw on a pair of black capris, a white cotton shirt and a comfortable pair of sandals. She quickly ran a comb through her hair, grabbed her purse and practically ran out the door. "Let's just get this over with," she grumbled.

It didn't take long to drive from her home to Toni's. Illuminated by a chandelier-style porch light, Mallory could see the home's elegant entrance and bright purple front door. *Impressive.* Toni's obviously made a lot of money.

Toni opened the door before Mallory had time to ring the bell. And so like Toni, she was wearing her signature purple scarf.

"Yes, I've done quite well," Toni boasted. "Come in."

Mallory took a quick glance at the expansive living room as Toni pulled her into her home office and ordered her to sit down. She wasted no time getting down to business. "Mallory, next time you see Forrest, you're going to tell him that painting is authentic."

"Toni, I can't do that. It isn't ethical."

"I don't care. You will do it."

The conversation became heated as Toni picked up a folder from the desk. It had Mallory's name in bold print across the tab. She pulled an envelope addressed to the FBI from the folder and waved it in Mallory's face.

"What's that?" Mallory asked.

"Just a lot of things the government should know you've done."

"Don't be such an ass, Toni. You know I haven't done anything."

"So, you say, but it'll take you a long time to get yourself untangled from the mess I'll put you in," Toni sneered.

"Are you telling me this is the only reason you wanted me here?" Mallory stood to leave.

"You're not going anywhere."

Toni angrily grabbed Mallory's arm, digging her nails into the soft flesh. Mallory tried to pull away but was not fast enough as Toni reached under her purple scarf and in one swift motion, flipped it over her head and onto Mallory's, pulling it down to her neck. As she stepped close to twist the scarf tight, Toni's foot became tangled in a throw rug. She lost her balance and went down hard, releasing her grip on the scarf. As she fell, her head smacked against the sharp corner of the desk. Mallory heard a hollow thud as Toni hit the floor. Within seconds blood pooled around Toni's head.

Oh my God! I've killed her, thought Mallory, as she tried without success to revive her. Finally, she understood Toni's heart had stopped and she was indeed dead.

What am I going to do now? Everyone will think this is my fault. This changes everything!

In a state of shock, Mallory grabbed her purse, ran out the front door and drove off in Monet. A million thoughts raced through her mind as she tried to decide what to do. *Shall I call the police? Should I tell Phebe? What am I going to do about Forrest?* Overwhelmed with dread, she somehow managed to arrive back at her home.

Hearing the driveway gate swing open with a familiar screech, Phebe awoke with a start and peered into the darkness. She could hear someone sobbing hysterically outside the casita near the pool area, could it be Mallory? Grabbing her phone, she quickly dashed off a text.

<pre>
Are you okay? Where have you been? Has
          something happened?
</pre>

With no response from Mallory, a now fully awake Phebe reached for her bathrobe and slippers. The glow from her bedside clock indicated it was 4:30 am.

As she left the casita and walked toward the main house to follow the mournful sound, Phebe found herself soaked in sweat, heart pounding, with a deep sense of dread. *What's going on?*

During Forrest's threatening phone call, Mallory had reluctantly promised she would drive up to his ranch to explain why the Ecke was a forgery. *Wait! Maybe what's happened to Mallory has something to do with Forrest!*

Worried, Phebe entered the kitchen through the unlocked door, climbed the back stairs to Mallory's room and pounded on her door several times. Mallory refused to invite her in, saying she didn't feel well and was going to stay in bed.

"Mallory! I heard you come in and I know something's

wrong. Please tell me what's going on. You can postpone your trip to Forrest's and resolve the forged Ecke issue another time. Look, you're exhausted and need to get some sleep. If you insist on driving up to the date ranch I can join you this afternoon."

In a weak, deflated voice, Mallory responded: "I have everything under control, Phebe. Don't worry. No need for you to come along. Go back to sleep. I'll be fine."

Phebe locked up Mallory's house and reluctantly returned to her casita, convinced something was very wrong with Mallory, but resigned to the fact she wasn't ready to talk about it.

Late that afternoon, Phebe tried once again to connect with Mallory, only to discover she had left the house and Monet was gone.

What was Mallory thinking? She knew calling on Forrest alone at night was risky. Yet she must've decided to go there anyway. *I should've stopped her.*

Phebe decided she'd check back once Mallory had returned. She told herself to relax. Mallory was a responsible adult who usually made good decisions.

CHAPTER 13

It was early evening by the time Mallory reached the turnoff at Old Woman Springs Road and headed to the date ranch.

She sighed. It was just as well she came alone after last night's horror with Toni. She'd barely made it home alive; her heart was still racing. How could she tell anyone what she had done? Pulling the turtleneck of her black sweater to her chin to hide the scratches and bruising on her neck, a tear slid down her cheek. *How will I survive in prison?*

She had to keep up appearances until she decided what to do. She'd meet with Forrest, collect the cost of her evaluation for the fake painting and get him to agree to a different sale so she could make a hefty commission. She'd now need it for a lawyer.

Forrest had been insistent, really threatening, about her coming at once after their phone conversation. He'd been less than thrilled to be told his Ecke was a fake.

The entire relationship between Forrest and Toni seemed off. How could Toni know so much about his date ranch? During her first visit, Toni had shared odd bits of information — like the white palm trees being date trees that don't bear fruit and were only used for land-scape projects. She said the water from the underground hot springs had to be cooled to use for irrigation. She'd stated no one knew how Forrest found this place or who he really was. Oddest of all, when Mallory asked Forrest for the painting's provenance, Toni, not Forrest, retrieved it from the drawer.

Something wasn't right. Mallory suspected Toni had sold him the painting at an inflated price and now that he realized it was a fake, he wanted to dump it on the highest bidder as soon as possible.

Why didn't he report her to the authorities? There must be something other than business between those two.

Mallory didn't like the idea of being alone with Forrest and was concerned about how he would greet her. He'd made a point of telling her Toni wouldn't be there this time. He couldn't know about last night, could he?

She had to be paid for her evaluation. Too bad it wasn't what Forrest and Toni expected. Something was fishy in this whole situation, but she didn't quite know what.

On a positive note, there was a painting she'd recog-nized on her previous visit and knew she could sell, if Forrest agreed. That sale would bring her a much-need-ed commission. And then there was the dagger squirreled away in the darkened hall. She had just caught a glimpse of it as they were walking through to the gallery. She was fairly sure it was Etruscan, which would date it to central Italy around the first century BC and make it extremely valuable. A similar piece had been stolen from the gallery where she and Toni had worked in New York. The insurance carrier had begrudgingly paid a high claim for that theft. Had it found its way to Forrest's collection? And if so, how? She needed to get a good look at that dagger and take some photos.

She could feel her heart pounding as Monet slowly cleared the guide rocks. Sweat trickled down her back from the nape of her neck. This had been much easier when Phebe directed her through these rocks. A scratch on her Lamborghini would be a repair she couldn't afford.

Bright flashes lit up the sky. Parking Monet, she felt the place was too quiet. It seemed deserted. Was it possible she drove all the way up here for nothing?

As she turned off the ignition, Forrest rushed from around the side of the house, turning his head to look over his shoulder.

"Come on in. Let's get down to business while we're alone. I can't believe your evaluation is correct. I was counting on that sale. Toni knows better than to cheat me."

Gathering her briefcase, Mallory followed Forrest into his home and into the now familiar gallery. Going straight to the painting, Mallory explained, "Now look here, Forrest. See how smooth the paint is? An original would have areas of texture; highs and lows in the thickness of the paint application. I'm confident in my decision; this is not original. I'm sorry if you feel you were cheated."

A thumping and scratching sound came from the back of the house — the same area from which Maria had appeared with that wonderful plate of cookies.

"I thought we were alone, Forrest."

"Don't worry about it. That was just the dogs."

Mallory opened her briefcase and pulled out a manila

folder. "This is my written report. I can't really call it an appraisal, as the painting isn't authentic." Turning to the last page of the report, she added, "Now that you know my rationale, I'd like to be paid for my work. Here's your bill."

Looking him in the eye, Mallory went on. "Forrest, I understand your disappointment. Maybe we can work something out. There's an oil painting, the one with partially clad women in a harem bath setting. You know the one? That painting is an original and valuable. I have a client I know would be interested and money is not an issue. If you would entertain selling that painting, I could forget the cost of this evaluation."

Mallory paused as she waited for Forrest to respond. "Please excuse me. I'd like to use the restroom; it was a long drive. Perhaps you'll give me an answer when I return."

She knew the dagger was in the floating glass case in the hall near the restroom. Stopping, she made sure the flash was set on her phone, and leaning over the case, she quickly snapped a picture. She would send it to the insurance company. If it was the stolen dagger, she was sure they'd pay way more for the information than any sales commission she might earn from Forrest.

Mallory was startled by that same scratching sound she'd heard earlier, followed by a distinct thump. It now seemed only feet away. Her nostrils flared as the sour smell of sweat drifted through the space. Tangled greying hair appeared first from the shadows, followed by the bent head of a short, swarthy man leaning on a cane.

"*Bonsoir.* I see you have a great appreciation for antiquities."

As he reached under the display case, she heard a click, and a bright light illuminated the objects inside. The case held much more than the dagger. As her eyes adjusted to the sudden light, she could see several small cylinder-shaped objects with intricately carved designs on them.

"Oh my God! Are these what I think they are?"

Rubbing his right thumb down a jagged scar on his cheekbone, the man answered. "Yes, Mallory, they are Mesopotamian cylinder seals from Iraq; used five thousand years ago to make an imprint, a signature of sorts, on property to uniquely identify the owner."

Mallory's eyes widened as the breath caught in her throat.

"Yes, I know your name and much more about you. Let us rejoin Forrest. We have much to talk about."

Stepping into the gallery, she could see Forrest casually leaning against the table looking over pictures of cylinder seals.

"I see you've met Rene, Rene Pascal."

"Forrest and I, and Toni, to be clear, have a little side business. We redistribute valuable artifacts to mostly billionaires. Millionaires have been priced out of the market," he chuckled.

"Yes," Forrest chimed in. "It has been very lucrative for all involved. Unfortunately, the woman who carried the seals to Mallorca for us had a few complications in her life. She died suddenly, leaving us without a courier for the most important sale."

"Toni told us about you," continued Rene. "We all agree you're knowledgeable, as you've proven. You present yourself well and you'd be accepted by our buyers. With no personal issues other than your financial demands, you'd be a good addition to our little enterprise.

This one trip could solve your financial problems for life. Too bad Toni isn't here while we explain it to you."

Half an hour later, a speechless Mallory was led to the door.

"We expect to hear a positive response from you within the next week. There are plans to be made for your trip to Mallorca. Time is money — a lot of money in this case!" Rene's voice lowered as he added, "Let me make myself clear. This information is to be shared with no one. Do you understand my meaning?"

Not trusting her voice, Mallory tipped her head forward, showing she did.

Hearing the door close behind her, she drew in a deep breath. She squinted, wrinkling her forehead, trying to see Monet through the pitch-black night. With shaking knees, Mallory walked toward the spot where she'd parked her. She had to get out of here, but Monet wasn't there. A bolt of lightning brightened the ranch, and she spotted her car parked on the side of the barn, about fifty yards from where she'd left her.

With no time to question how Monet had been moved, she rushed forward. Her path alternated from pitch black to over bright, as the storm intensified.

Pressing the key fob to unlock the car, she heard the crunch of footsteps behind her. Turning in the direction of the sound, she felt a searing pain at the back of her neck, and everything went dark.

CHAPTER 14

Mallory slowly began to regain consciousness. Disoriented and with a mounting sense of fear, she wondered where she was and what had happened to her.

Ouch! My head hurts! I can't open my eyes or move my arms. Why am I here? What's going on?

As her mind began to clear, Mallory understood she was blindfolded and tied up in a tight space. Frantic, she gasped, trying to suck in air, grateful she could breathe at all with the cloth blindfold pressed against her lips. Rough unyielding rope gnawed at her hands and ankles. Her feet had gone numb.

I'm being held captive! But by whom? And why me? I've gotta get out of here.

Mallory began to panic, finally realizing she was trapped with no way to escape. Shaking with fear, she reminded herself to breathe. Years ago her yoga teacher had taught her a technique to restore calm.

If you want to clear your head, she'd said, focus on the breath; breathe in and out. Unsure if it would work, but knowing she'd have to relax before she could help herself, Mallory willed herself to ease her tight muscles. Five counts, inhale … five counts hold … five counts, release the breath. Repeat and continue. After a few moments, she found it easier to focus.

Her first priority was to try to loosen the blindfold and the ropes that bound her. She began gently rolling her head back and forth, but discovered the blindfold wouldn't budge. She raised, lowered and attempted to twist her shoulders to expand her range of motion. In doing so, she began to sense the cramped space she occupied seemed oddly familiar. Moving her butt and legs took effort, but proved futile. Sniffing the air, she caught a whiff of her favorite fragrance — YSL Opium.

Why would this space smell like me?

With a flash of insight, Mallory wondered, *Could this be the front passenger seat of my beloved Monet? Is it possible I'm being held prisoner in my own car?*

Thinking back, she remembered driving Monet to the high desert to meet Forrest at his home. She couldn't recall whether that happened just a few minutes ago or last week. At this moment, she had no concept of time or place.

My God! she thought. *What was I thinking, to drive all the way up to Forrest's after what happened with Toni? Wait a minute … Toni's dead!*

Her memories of the night with Toni caused bile to rise in her throat. *What have I done? Maybe what's happening to me now is a strange kind of karma.*

More memories flooded her consciousness. She recalled the scene at the date ranch, with Forrest's nonsense about the fake painting being authentic and Toni cheating him. Then, out of nowhere, there was that weird old Frenchman and his threats. She wondered who he was and how he knew so much about her. The only reason Forrest summoned her in the first place was to authenticate a painting — nothing else.

How did that creepy old man get involved with Forrest and Toni?

She recalled her horror hearing their scheme to recruit her as a courier. Too frightened to tell them she wanted no part of their plans, she simply listened until she could safely make an exit.

She remembered walking out the front door toward her car, and that Monet wasn't where she'd left her. It had started to storm, so she'd raced ahead through the mud and pouring rain. When she opened Monet's door, something smacked her on the head from behind. Could it have been Forrest?

Approaching footsteps now startled Mallory out of her reverie and her heart began to pound in her chest. Thump! Thump! Thump!

Oh my God! Someone's coming. I'd better play possum — it may be my only chance of surviving this nightmare!

Mallory again slowed her breathing and tried to relax. The driver's side door swung open and the odor of old sweat and tobacco entered the vehicle. Monet sagged with the weight of this new arrival, who seemed large, even oafish. An elbow jabbed her bruised shoulder. Despite her efforts to be still, she cringed and groaned.

"Are you awake?" a male voice whispered in her ear.

Mallory remained unmoving — frozen, not recognizing the voice. *Who is this guy and what's he got against me?*

"In a little while, we'll take a hike together and I'll leave you in a place where no one will find you." As he spoke, he jammed a needle into Mallory's arm.

"I've always wanted a Lamborghini." His voice began to fade as the drug began to take hold. "Now I'll be driving a sexy yellow one to Mexico," he added, making an odd giggling noise that sent tremors up and down Mallory's spine. "You may die. I don't know. Can't help it. Sorry."

The engine roared and the radio blasted as the man now had full control of Monet. Fleetwood Mac's, "Don't Stop Thinking about Tomorrow," filled the night air, as the car climbed the hill to enter Joshua Tree National Park.

"Good. As I suspected, no one's at the checkpoint at this hour," he muttered.

Fighting to stay conscious, Mallory felt the car flying through the dark, but was powerless to react. Convinced the man was driving well over the speed limit on the dark curvy road, her panic was at the breaking point. They continued through the park until he rasped, "Pinto Basin Road," and made a right turn. At this point, Mallory could no longer fight the effects of the drug she'd been given and finally surrendered to the darkness.

The car cruised down the hill to Cottonwood Springs, where the driver turned off the road. He knew a spot where the car wouldn't be seen. Stopping, he turned off the ignition, flung the door open and jumped out. He opened the passenger door, hoisted Mallory's limp body over his shoulder and headed up the trail. The hike to Mastodon Mine was easy for him, since it was a familiar place he and his father had often visited when he was a boy. He remembered how they would look for gold, and pretend they'd found enough to explore the world together.

Arriving at the entrance to the mine, the man set

Mallory down and leaned her against a large boulder. He bent over to pick up a small tree branch that had fallen to the ground. Walking to an alcove in the wall, he used the branch as a broom to clear a space for her body. Satisfied with his efforts, he then returned to carry Mallory into the mine and place her in the area he had prepared.

Looking at her body as he loosened the binding from Mallory's arms and legs, he leaned over to smooth her hair and decided something was missing. He left the mine and searched until he spotted a creosote bush with yellow blossoms. He then snapped off a sprig and carried it into the mine, nestling the blossoms in her hands and arranging them across her chest.

"If you're as tough as this bush, there's a chance you'll survive … for a little while, anyway." That done, he hurried back to the car. He squeezed his bulk into the Lamborghini, gunned it, and disappeared into the night.

CHAPTER 15

The next morning, when Mallory still hadn't returned, a guilt-ridden Phebe called Emily and explained the situation.

Emily calmed Phebe's fears. "You know, Phebe, Mallory's a strong, fearless woman who knows how to take care of herself. I noticed there was a lightning storm up there last night. Mallory probably rode out the storm at a hotel in Joshua Tree or Yucca Valley. You can expect her to call any minute to check in."

Still uneasy, but less worried now that she had spoken with Emily, Phebe made herself some coffee, looked at her calendar and mapped out her day.

A few hours later, when Mallory had neither returned nor called, Phebe texted Dana.

Have you heard from Mallory? She met with Forrest Williams last night at the date ranch and still hasn't returned.

Dana responded:

No word from Mallory. Have you called Forrest to see when she left his place?

Phebe replied:

I don't have his information, so I have no
way to get ahold of him.

Grabbing Mallory's spare house key from a hook near the front door, Phebe rushed over and entered the main house, hoping to find anything that would help her get in touch with Forrest. Finally, she found his name and phone number scribbled on a notepad near Mallory's land line. She immediately called Forrest, whose voicemail picked up.

"Forrest. This is Phebe, Mallory's friend, who visited you earlier this week. Mallory didn't return home last night, and I wondered what time she left your place. Please call me back."

That afternoon, Phebe decided to rally the troops and invited Dana and Emily to join her at the casita for drinks and appetizers.

"Okay. It's 5 o'clock and still no word from Mallory. She's been gone at least twenty-four hours," said Phebe. "What are your thoughts?"

"I don't know what to think," replied Dana, taking a big gulp of her wine. "Mallory's super responsible. She would've called by now."

"Should we call the police?" asked Emily.

Phebe paused before answering. "Anyone who's ever watched *Law and Order* knows the police won't do anything until an adult's been missing forty-eight hours."

"Yeah. We've heard that." Dana and Emily agreed.

"We have to do something," groaned Phebe. "She was crying when she came home late last night. She was acting secretive and wouldn't talk to me. She said she wasn't feeling well. What if she's seriously sick or has been in an accident? Or, heaven forbid, met with foul play!"

After a moment, Emily had an idea.

"Do you remember that guy, Arthur something, who was at the séance? He was the distinguished-looking older man who'd recently lost his wife."

The others nodded. They remembered him.

"When we were here a while back during Modernism Week with all the house tours, Dana and I noticed Arthur in the crowd outside and he was wearing a uniform. While we were driving through all the tourists, we waved at him, but I don't think he saw us. The patch on his uniform said, 'Citizens on Patrol' and he and another guy looked like they were doing traffic control."

"And … this has to do with Mallory's situation, how?" asked Phebe.

"Well, since we can't file a missing persons report for another twenty-four hours, we can at least call Arthur, find out more about what he does for the police, and share our concerns. He may have some ideas on what we can do next. He may also have a good connection with someone on the force who would take us seriously."

"Great idea, Emily," said Phebe. "I got one of Arthur's business cards at the cafe in Idyllwild." She began looking in her purse, and after rummaging around, found it. "Here it is. I'll call him right now."

Arthur answered immediately. Delighted to hear from her, he was happy to listen and assist. Phebe asked him if he was available to come to the casita right then, and he accepted without hesitation.

Twenty minutes later, Arthur was sitting in the casita's living room. Phebe proceeded to describe the Mallory situation in great detail, starting with Mallory's first encounter with Forrest and Toni at the Hanson Gallery event. Emily and Dana chimed in with details when they could. When Phebe finished, she asked Arthur what he thought.

Arthur's analytical mind was working overtime. He paused for a moment and cleared his throat before speaking.

"Phebe. Ladies. This situation is disturbing and you're right to be concerned. Your friend could be in great danger. Do you mind if I ask you some questions and take notes?"

"Not at all," replied Phebe.

Arthur spent almost an hour writing down details of the situation, along with contact information for Forrest and phone numbers for Mallory and Toni. No one in the group had an address for Toni, but they were able to retrieve her phone number and email address, based on a brochure she'd given Emily at the Hanson Gallery.

"This is a good start," said Arthur, standing up to leave. "I'll make some inquiries at the station and speak with Dave Elliott, a personal friend and one of the best detectives I know. Please continue your efforts to contact Mallory and Mr. Williams. He sounds like a pretty unsavory character! If we can't locate Mallory tomorrow, I'll meet you at the station around 5:00 pm and you can file a missing persons report."

"Thank you, Arthur. You've been a big help," said Dana.

Just as Arthur opened the sliding door to exit the casita, he suddenly paused and turned around. His face was grim.

"Is there something else, Arthur? You look like you've seen a ghost," asked Emily.

"I just had a disturbing thought about our medium from the séance in Idyllwild. Do you remember what she said when she canceled the séance?"

"That's something I'll never forget," responded Phebe. "Soon, one of you will die and another in this room will stand trial for murder. Oh my God! You don't think there's any connection, do you? Is Mallory's life in danger?"

"Let's not get carried away until we have some solid evidence. It still strikes me as something worth throwing into the mix, no matter how far-fetched it seems."

After Arthur left, the three women reviewed their next actions. Dana would continue researching Forrest Williams. She also offered to find out more about the devious Toni Vitale and try to get a home address for her. Phebe said she would continue calling and texting Forrest, Mallory and Toni. Emily would contact Arthur Webster for updates every few hours.

Exhausted after a long, stressful day, they concluded their evening, went their separate ways and promised to stay in touch.

The next morning, after another sleepless night and no word from Mallory, Phebe was frantic with worry. The day seemed to drag on endlessly and produced no news. At 5:00, the three friends finally got into Emily's car and drove to the Palm Springs Police Department to meet Arthur and file a missing persons report.

The Palm Springs Police Department, located just off

Tahquitz Canyon Way near the airport, was just a short distance from Mallory's house. That afternoon the skies were filled with noise from military jets doing routine training runs over the Coachella Valley. When Phebe, Dana and Emily arrived, Arthur greeted them in the lobby. He introduced them to Detective Dave Elliott, who sat them down, listened to their account of Mallory's disappearance, and helped them file a missing person's report, while Arthur hovered nearby.

Finally, the detective agreed the situation was troublesome and promised he would start an investigation immediately. Before the women left, he gave each one his business card, including his personal cell phone number, and encouraged them to call him any time if they thought of anything they'd left out or if they came upon any new information.

CHAPTER 16

Pascal leaned heavily on his cane as he approached the display case for a private look at the cylinder seals. He'd risked his life getting his hands on these beauties.

That stinking museum. It was hot as hell as they'd crawled through blown-out rooms and narrow stairways littered with shattered glass and destroyed antiquities. He didn't give these a second glance. He was after what he could carry easily --- the cylinder seals. He'd paid a museum director a small fortune in advance, something he'd never done before, for access. Abu had been a fixture at the museum for decades, undervalued and taken for granted by other museum personnel. However, he'd been trusted with the keys for years. Abu knew the seals were in lockers in a basement room. More importantly, he knew which unmarked keys opened which unmarked doors and which brown storage lockers contained the seals. They'd made their way to the room but couldn't see the lockers through the darkness. Someone had the idea to light the room by setting fire to discarded black packing foam. They had only half-filled one backpack when the air became too noxious to continue. In their rush to escape the fumes, Abu dropped the keys. There would be no second attempt. He'd gotten out but knew his borrowed Iraqi uniform wouldn't fool anyone for long. With horror he noticed the blood running down his left pant leg.

Standing next to the hallway's entrance, Forrest could see the exhaustion on Pascal's face. He appeared to be daydreaming as he looked at the last of their seals in the display case.

These ancient cylinder seals were highly prized. About the size of an index finger, artisans carved them from carnelian and lapis lazuli. Each seal had been worn around the neck of a wealthy citizen living in ancient Mesopotamia. Forrest closed his eyes and visualized himself wearing one of the ornate artifacts. He knew they were priceless pieces of history, and this final buyer had agreed to pay a fortune to include them in his collection.

In Iraq, Forrest had watched Pascal wrap the seals and he'd helped by paying soldiers to stow these packages in their duffle bags. The soldiers were willing to carry them on board their military flights home. They'd asked no questions and were happy to deposit the packages in an airport locker.

Forrest anticipated receiving a reward from Rene for his loyalty and for securing the seals at the date ranch -- perhaps even a fifty-fifty split. Imagining he'd be a wealthy man before long, he let out an audible sigh.

Pascal turned, becoming aware of Forrest's presence. "Forrest, take me someplace where I can have a stiff drink. I feel like a caged lion cooped up here."

Forrest thought of Rene as his friend and equal, unaware Pascal thought of him only as a minion, to do his bidding.

"There are several good watering holes in Palm Springs."

"Let's get the hell out of here. I want a good bottle of scotch sitting in front of me. Or a Ricard if I can get it."

Entering the dimly lit bar and choosing a corner table opposite the wall-mounted TV, they noticed only one other patron sitting at a table in the middle of the room. It reeked with the odor of stale beer, which had soaked into the wooden floor over the years. Pascal settled for a double Chivas. Forrest ordered the same.

"Good time to bring you up to speed on what's been going on since Martine's death," Forrest began. "The coroner ruled her death a heart attack. It was no heart attack," he smirked. Forrest knew Pascal would be pleased with this information.

Pascal was never in the same place for more than a week or so. He was continually traveling from country to country for his business ventures or to stay ahead of the law, or both. He looked so tired. Maybe he's looking for someone to take over part of his vast and lucrative empire, mused Forrest.

"She thought she was hidden from me, even when she moved to the States. She'd married, and changed her name, even losing contact with her sister for years. I followed her every move and could have arranged for her to see Nicole if she'd asked."

Pascal continued. "She'd done an excellent job moving our antiquities and our buyers liked her. When she refused my repeated requests to continue working for us, I knew she had to be eliminated. She knew too much."

"Yes, I agree," said Forrest. Martine's death had caused a major disruption in Pascal's plans.

Taking a loud gulp of his Chivas, Pascal changed the subject. "How's Toni doing? Have you seen her lately? I thought you might marry her." He was tired and began slurring his words.

"Well, Toni agreed to have the baby, and give him to me. Thinking back, I have no idea why I took him. Buddy's been nothing but a headache, pack of troubles. He's a big bruiser and drugged out most of the time. He lives in a room off the barn. His favorite meal is a case of cheap beer. Not sure when he's sober. Wish I could give him back. Buddy doesn't know Toni's his mother. She made it obvious she hates kids."

"Where is he now?"

"Rene, I don't know. I can't waste time worrying about him. He's been gone for a while. Said he was going to Mexico. But he's full of crazy ideas. He doesn't have a passport and where he gets his money is a mystery to me. Probably dealing drugs."

Although he'd asked about Toni, Pascal was bored listening to Forrest drone on about Buddy. "I didn't come all the way from Mallorca to listen to this shit."

"Mallory is a good substitute for Martine. When I met her at the ranch and explained our proposal, she was extremely interested in the money. Has she agreed yet?"

"I don't know. Toni said she would talk to her and get back to me."

"When was the last time you talked with Toni?"

"I haven't heard from her in a couple of days."

The man sitting at the center table raised his glass and whistled at the cocktail waitress. "I'll have another, honey, and I'd like you to join me."

"My husband will have it ready right away. He's the bartender."

"Oops! Look at the time. Gotta go," he announced sheepishly and quickly departed.

Just then, the bartender turned on the TV to a blaring news alert about a missing woman.

"Listen up, Pascal! They could be talking about Mallory. The reporter said a local woman was found in Joshua Tree. That's near the ranch. She was airlifted to Desert Regional, in serious condition. My God, we'd better talk to Toni now!"

"You know where she lives."

Arriving at Toni's home, Forrest led the way to the purple door and was surprised to find it ajar. He pushed the door wide open and let Pascal enter before him. Even with the air conditioning, the house reeked of an intense odor.

"*Mon Dieu!* Forrest, that smells like a dead body, rotting meat. *Tres mal.*"

The two, drawn by the stench, cautiously made their way down the hall and into Toni's office, where they found her lying on the floor in a pool of blood. The putrid smell of death emanated from her body and permeated the air.

Pascal took out a handkerchief to cover his nose and mouth "How long do you think she's been dead?"

"From the stench, at least three days."

"Could Bud have done this to Toni? Or could he be the one who hurt Mallory?"

"He was obsessed with Mallory's car, but that wouldn't have anything to do with Toni. I doubt he even knows where Toni lives."

"Don't touch anything. Let's get the hell out. *Allons.*

Vite, vite." Pascal was already retracing his steps to the purple door.

Forrest started the engine. "Maybe Mallory knows something about this. We could send her flowers and pay her a visit at the hospital. Or I could call the police or the newscaster."

"*Mon Dieu. Non, non Forrest. No gendarmes.*" Pascal was adamant, swearing to himself in French. "Don't contact anyone. I want to get the seals into my buyer's hands within the next couple of weeks. With Mallory in the hospital, we'll have to change our plan. We'll have to rely on the news and talk to no one."

"Maybe a nurse could tell us something."

"Forrest, did you hear me? Pascal slammed his fist on the dashboard. "No one."

CHAPTER 17

This is the most "normal" thing I've done in months, Brad thought as he drove east on Tahquitz Canyon Way toward Chuck's office. It had been a couple of years since he and his younger brother had seen each other face-to-face. Both were eager to spend time together and catch up. Chuck had suggested lunch at Pomme Frite, because he knew Brad liked Belgian food.

As he drove past Sherman's Deli, Brad shrugged, reminding himself this was the life he'd chosen after graduating from university with degrees in international economics and law. After passing the bar, he joined the Drug Enforcement Administration, where he'd worked — mostly undercover — for the past twenty-five years. Though dangerous, Brad loved his work and knew he was doing something important for his country. It was his job with the DEA that brought him to the Coachella Valley three months ago.

Brad had been following a lead on a drug operation connected to an international syndicate based somewhere in the Mediterranean. The local connection was reputed to be Alex Dunbar, a sketchy guy from New Orleans. Brad had been tracking Dunbar in Louisiana until he suddenly disappeared, turning up later in the Coachella Valley. Dunbar was just a low-level operator in the organization, but it was probable he knew useful information that could lead up the chain to the whereabouts of notorious kingpin, Rene Pascal.

Pascal, a big player in international crime, was legendary for drug and sex trafficking. His obsession with stolen antiquities was a lucrative sideline that added to his immense wealth. His whereabouts hadn't been confirmed in over a decade.

The search for Alex Dunbar hit a snag when Brad discovered Dunbar was now known as Annalore Dubois and supplemented her income as a medium leading séances and as a performer in local drag shows. In fact, Brad, using his real name but one of his more ridiculous undercover personas, had recently attended one of Annalore's séances in a local mountain resort.

Unfortunately, Annalore had abruptly canceled the séance and disappeared before he could talk with her. Undeterred, Brad fruitlessly spent the next few weeks searching for her and anyone else in her network.

Turning right on Calle El Segundo, then making an immediate left, he entered the parking garage behind the FBI field office. Yes, my little brother has done all right for himself, he thought, parking his black SUV.

Chuck Merrill had followed his older brother into law enforcement and had traveled the world investigating art forgeries. He'd built a solid reputation as an agent and was respected among his colleagues. Recently in Europe, he'd been injured in a failed attempt to take down the world's most successful art forgery team.

During the raid, Chuck had been shot, hospitalized and put on leave while he convalesced. When he was declared fit enough, the FBI sent him to Palm Springs to provide his expertise for an ongoing investigation. Palm Springs had recently been identified as a major hub for the sale of stolen art.

Entering the FBI's front door, Brad was immediately struck by how small the office was. A friendly receptionist greeted him, checked his bona fides and called Chuck, who came out to escort him to the back, where his office was located.

"Hey, little bro. How's it going?" greeted Brad, giving his brother a big hug.

"I've been better, but things are starting to look up," replied Chuck, all smiles.

"That's the spirit. It looks like you're putting in the work — doing your physical therapy and letting your body heal. Have you talked to someone about healing your psyche?"

"Yep. I wasn't much interested, but my boss forced me. I have to say, it's helped a lot."

"That's all good, Chuck. It sounds like you're doing everything right. Are you still up for lunch?"

"You bet," replied Chuck, reaching for his wallet and cell phone. "The restaurant's not far away, so we can take advantage of this glorious weather and walk. I'm sure you'll like it."

As the brothers exited through a moderately spacious bullpen, Brad mused: *Even the great FBI has succumbed to a world of cubicles.* A sudden movement caught Brad's attention and made him look to his left. Working on a computer at the farthest cubicle was someone who looked familiar.

That's weird, thought Brad. I could swear that guy is the young man who befriended the grieving couple at the séance. What in the world is he doing here? He presented himself as a student at the local community college. I'll definitely have to ask Chuck about him.

Later Brad and Chuck were seated in the quaint sidewalk bistro, enjoying cold glasses of pinot gris with the restaurant's specialty — a baker's dozen black mussels on the half shell, oven baked, au gratin style. As they dined, they happily reminisced about their shared childhood and caught up on more recent activities.

"Remember when you convinced me I could fly if I jumped off the hayloft and flapped my arms?" asked Chuck.

"I swear I didn't know you would actually do it."

"So you say. It's a miracle I survived."

"The only injuries I noticed were to your fragile ego!"

Finally, Chuck asked, "Brad, you've been married to your work forever. While you say it's been rewarding, haven't you missed out on a personal life? Isn't it about time you found someone special and settled down?"

Brad paused for a moment before he spoke. "Chuck, you're a fine one to be giving me relationship advice, since you're in the same boat! You know I've had plenty of female companionship over the years and I've enjoyed every bit of it. With the kind of work I do, I never felt it would be fair to bring any woman into my crazy world for the long term. I sometimes wonder if I'm even capable of sharing my life."

"As you well know, Brad, I'm almost ten years younger

than you, and even with the job and my injuries, I've managed to maintain a healthy, long-term relationship with Vanessa. I imagine we'll marry soon. I'm more concerned you'll end up a sad old bachelor with a cat, reliving your past glories in a squalid studio apartment in DC."

Brad laughed at the thought of the dismal future Chuck envisioned.

"Actually, Chuck, over the past couple of weeks, I've been thinking the same thing. I'm getting close to retirement and I'm pretty well fixed financially. I'd love to find a permanent home — maybe here in the desert — where I'd be free to travel, take up a hobby, and even get a dog. I recently met an intriguing woman who is beautiful, inside and out."

"Now you're talking! Let me know where that leads," encouraged Chuck.

"You'll be the first to know," promised Brad. "On another subject, when I walked through your office, I recognized a young man I've seen before working at one of the computers. He appears to be of mixed race, has dark curly hair and wears glasses. Today he's wearing a plain blue button-down shirt. He seems awfully young to be working for the FBI."

"Oh, right. That's Lance Harris. He works in the FBI's Antiquities Division and is here on temporary assignment. He's new and looks like a teenager, but he has a great reputation and is considered a bit of a genius in his specialty. In fact, we're working together on a big project right now. Where have you seen him before?"

"I'm afraid I can't give details until I clear it with HQ, but something isn't adding up and I'd like to investigate further. It's possible we're working on similar cases. Does the name, Rene Pascal, mean anything to you?"

That name hung ominously in the air for a few beats. Finally, Chuck spoke.

"Let me know what HQ has to say as soon as you can. We're pursuing something big and dangerous, involving some really bad people."

"Will do." Brad paused and then continued. "Okay, we're having a nice lunch in a fabulous resort town. Let's move on to more pleasant topics. Can you suggest any sightseeing here in the Coachella Valley? Or has it just been work, work, work?"

The brothers visited a few minutes more, finished their lunch and walked back to the field office.

"Let's do this again soon," said Chuck. After giving Brad a brotherly hug, he entered the building.

Brad responded with a thumbs-up, but his mind was elsewhere as he walked to his vehicle in the parking structure.

CHAPTER 18

Dave Elliott stood to stretch his back and hike up the tightening waist of his "gardening pants," as Joan called them. Though he was grateful for the cool evening air, he still had to wipe the sweat that had run down from his dense gray hair. His weight had ballooned in the past year, even though he continued spending his evenings tending Joan's vegetable garden. He always intended to eat more of the lettuce, tomatoes and peppers, but invariably passed them out at the office and picked up a takeout meal for himself.

He'd been on the job nearly twenty-five years. They had been very frugal with their money and Joan had planned a trip around the world for the two of them. They would leave right after his retirement party. That didn't happen. She was diagnosed with cancer and died four months later. Now entering his twenty-seventh year, he had no desire to spend time alone on a vacation, opting for the daily grind he was familiar with.

A man of discipline, he rinsed the gardening tools and stored them in the shed Joan had helped him build. The hose supplied water to cool his head and clean his hands before he entered the house. Pulling the handle on the patio door, it stuck, another thing he'd been meaning to fix. He entered the kitchen and opened the fridge to snag a Modelo Negra.

Taking the beer back to the patio, he admired the rich amber color as he poured it into a beer stein. He liked that the taste started sweet like apples only to end with the slight bitterness of hops. Just like life.

It had been an uneventful day until Arthur brought the women in.

He and Arthur had become close as both had lost their wives suddenly. Arthur would not accept that his wife Martine had died of a heart attack. She'd told him of her experience while still a college student. Through her sister Nicole, she'd met and been forced to smuggle artifacts, among other illegal activities, for a Frenchman living in Mallorca, named Pascal. Martine had changed her identity and was able to elude him for years. However, several months ago, he'd found her, and wanted her to continue as before. Pascal told her Nicole wanted to see her and although she was concerned for her sister, Martine was scared and refused. Arthur acknowledged she hadn't given him many details, saying she felt he would be safer not knowing. She'd been a strong vibrant woman with no health issues.

Arthur was insistent she couldn't have died from a heart attack and her death must have had something to do with this smuggler. Detective Elliott did not discount Arthur's feelings and knew from experience if something nefarious was to blame for Martine's death it would come to light at some point.

Arthur had come into the office this afternoon, something he often did just to chat. But, today had been different. Arthur introduced him to Phebe, Emily, and Dana. Their friend Mallory had gone missing, and they wanted to file a report. They hadn't heard anything from her for over 48 hours. Dave believed the circumstance of her disappearance was suspicious and agreed to investigate. He'd let them know as soon as he heard anything.

Filing the report before he left would ensure the next shift would see it.

Something was bothering him about the information the women had supplied. Something in the report seemed familiar, but he couldn't quite figure out what it was. Instead of waiting until tomorrow morning to start the inquiry, he made several calls as he sipped his beer. Charlie, the Riverside County Coroner, said they had no bodies matching Mallory's description. This was good news. High Desert Medical Center, the nearest hospital to Joshua Tree National Park, had only admitted a couple of rock climbers in their early twenties.

The trauma center at Desert Regional also had nothing to report, but promised to get back to him if anything changed.

Opening another beer, he settled down in his Lazy Boy recliner and switched to the PBS channel on the TV. Lulled by the droning voice in the documentary, he set the sleep timer for ninety minutes, knowing the silence would wake him for the eleven o'clock local news. It did, and there was nothing relating to the missing woman. Wanting to touch all bases, he called the station's after-hours line, explained who he was and asked for a call back if a woman matching Mallory's description made the news for any reason. The person on the other end of the conversation seemed distracted. He'd call back in the morning when the old timers were in the newsroom.

At his desk the next afternoon, after he stretched his neck, rolled his head side to side, front to back, round and round to relieve the stiffness brought on by last night's deep sleep in the recliner, he decided to head out for a burger. Passing the break room, he caught a glimpse of the banner running across the bottom of the TV screen. Breaking News, Breaking News.

On the screen was Kelly, the local reporter.

Standing among boulders near a parking lot, her auburn hair whipping around her face, she was interviewing a man and woman and what looked like two kids jumping around in the background.

"I'm here at Joshua Tree National Monument with visitors from Michigan, the Nelsons."

Holding tight to the microphone, she aimed it just under the nose of a tall, scraggly, bearded man. "Can you tell me what happened up here this morning, Mr. Nelson?"

"Well, we got up here early. We wanted to hike to Mastodon Mine with the boys. It was their first time and Betty and I thought they'd be thrilled. We told them it was an old gold mine, and they might even find some valuable nuggets. They didn't fall for that story even after we told them we'd go to McDonald's when we got back."

"Yes, that's interesting," shouted reporter Kelly over the howl of wind. "but what did you find?"

Not wanting to lose even a minute of his fifteen minutes of fame, the bearded one continued. "You know kids -- first they didn't want to go, too much hiking uphill, then downhill, over a ravine and boulders. The trail was really narrow between some cliffs. They were hungry, this was boring. Then they decided to take off running. Wasn't long before we lost sight of them. Then we heard them shouting and screaming, so Betty and I took off at a run, not knowing what they'd gotten into."

Just behind the reporter, two boys could be seen. Their arms interlocked, they nearly toppled over as they were kicking wildly at each other. A dark-haired woman ran through the scene waving her arms and punching her fist to the sky.

Kelly reached out to a uniformed arm that could be seen nearly off camera. "Officer, can I get a statement from you?"

"Nope, sorry. No time."

She moved the mic back for the continuing story from Mr. Nelson.

"As we came around the bend, Johnny was pointing to the mouth of the cave shouting, "There's a dead body in there!""

Betty approached the reporter, tired of trying to corral the boys. She pulled the microphone from the beard and continued the story. "You could tell they were scared, rooted in place they were. I gathered them to me while Burt went into the mine. It wasn't two minutes before he came rushing out, hollering, "Call 911! A woman in there is unconscious and barely alive!""

"I gave him water from my backpack along with the boys' extra tee shirts we seem to always need."

Burt eased the mic back saying, "I went back in and wiped the lady's face and whispered to her that help was on the way. She didn't respond, didn't even move. It was freaky. She was laid out like a corpse. Her hands were folded across her chest with weeds in them. I thought she was a goner for sure.

"An ambulance and police cars showed up, but they couldn't get their equipment through the narrow path. It wasn't long before a helicopter flew in, but wasn't able to land. Not enough flat space in that parking lot. I guess it was from the marine base at Twenty-Nine Palms. I think that's close. We didn't know what was going to happen to the poor woman.

"Finally, they dropped a medic down on a rope from the chopper. That was something. The boys loved that. Next thing we can see, they secured her to a basket and lifted her up. Then the chopper flew off.

"The officers asked if we checked for identification. I said we didn't want to move her and didn't see any identification. My wife took a picture of her, mainly because of the police shows she watches on TV. She sent it to Sergeant Vasquez, the man in charge, along with our contact information.

"Sergeant Vasquez made a big deal of congratulating the boys for finding the woman and thanked us for our quick actions. He said we were all heroes and if the woman lived, she could thank us for finding her. He said he'd personally let us know how she was doing. That was nice."

Betty added, "He also said they'd searched the mine and its surroundings and hadn't found a single clue, other than a large shoe print."

The wind blew up dust as two police cars and an ambulance could be seen maneuvering to turn around in the parking lot, then drove off. The boys ran past, shouting, "Big Mac and fries!"

The program shifted to a commercial and Dave decided to check with Desert Regional again and put in a call to

Sergeant Vasquez to have the woman's picture sent to him before he called Dana and Arthur. They may have seen the same news report.

CHAPTER 19

Hi, Arthur. This is Dana. I have you on speaker. Emily and I are having lunch at Phebe's. Have you heard anything from Detective Elliott? We just saw Kelly's newscast."

"Yes, Dana. I saw it too and was about to call him."

Dana sounded breathless as though she'd been running. "They found a woman in a cave up at Joshua Tree. We know Mallory went up to see Forrest and when she didn't return, we were afraid she may have been in an accident or driven off the road. She was really tired. But being found in Joshua Tree National Park in a cave; if it's Mallory, something terrible must have happened."

"I'll ask Dave to call you directly. If you don't mind, I'd like to join the three of you so we can be together when he calls. I can be there in less than five minutes."

"Yes, do come over."

"Please stay calm. We don't know it's Mallory."

Arthur arrived just as Detective Elliott's call came in. He told them Officer Vasquez had confirmed the air lift was for an unconscious woman. He gave a general description of her, saying no identification was found. Unfortunately, a picture taken at the scene was too blurry and dark to make out, so an in-person identification would be needed. The woman was taken to Desert Regional. Vasquez also said she had been laid out in a manner that would indicate an expectant death. He doubted she did this to herself, as a large footprint was found in the cave, despite indications someone had tried to erase it. An investigation had been opened.

Detective Elliott told them Vasquez's information had been relayed to hospital personnel. The nurse in charge confirmed they would be allowed access for identification purposes. She stressed there was to be no noise. Her staff needed time to stabilize the patient. She suggested they check with Emergency Admitting later that evening to make an identification.

When Dana, Phebe and Detective Elliott entered the Emergency area at Desert Regional, Phebe noticed Emily wasn't with them.

A few minutes later, the automatic doors made a whooshing sound as Emily entered, pulling her light sweater tight across her chest. The smell of disinfectant overpowered her nostrils, and the cold from a cranked-up air conditioning system added to her discomfort. She pushed back the unpleasant memories that threatened to unnerve her. Emily would close those back in their drawer, as she'd learned to compartmentalize over the years. Mallory was more important now.

Turning her head to the sound of a deep moan, Emily saw a disheveled man with a blood-soaked towel wrapped around his hand. Determined not to be triggered by anything she heard or saw in this hospital; she consciously took a deep breath and slowly released it through her mouth.

"Ladies, please find a seat. I'll let them know we're here." Detective Elliott's voice brought Emily back to the purpose of this visit.

"I think I'll stand," said Dana as she noticed Emily's complexion had become more pale than usual. "Are you okay, Emily? Maybe you'd like to sit down."

"Yes, please sit," agreed Phebe.

Detective Elliott returned. "They have her in a secure room off the corridor, next to the Emergency wing."

A white-clad nurse approached. "Please come this way," she instructed, as she led them through the Emergency wing and down the corridor.

Emily looked neither left nor right.

The nurse opened the door to one of two rooms on the right side of the corridor and escorted them in. "Please don't stay too long. I'll be waiting outside. We have much more to do for her." As she left, she flipped the door stopper down, preventing the door from closing all the way.

The person lying on the bed looked so small and helpless. Tubes inserted into her nose and mouth were attached to clear canisters. There were three IV bags hanging from an upright rack, with the fluid barely used. The woman in the bed was Mallory.

Phebe gasped at the sight of her friend. She was dressed in a clean pink hospital gown, which was at odds with the rest of her appearance. Her hair was matted and crusted against her head. The area around the IV site had been cleaned but not the rest of her arm. Her fingernails were ragged, the polish nearly gone. Dirt mixed with what looked like dry blood nestled in the crease of her neck. The only clean part of her body was her face. It was Mallory to be sure.

"Yes, it's Mallory" they all whispered.

Detective Elliott nodded, acknowledging their identification just as the door swung open and the nurse came back into the room. She was followed by an orderly pushing a gurney.

"We need to take her for tests now. I'm glad you found your friend. You can wait if you'd like; it may be an hour or so. If you let the volunteers at the desk know where you'll be, I'll find you when she's back in her room. Keep in mind you won't be able to stay more than fifteen minutes, and she may not regain consciousness. If any of you have access to her medical identification and driver's license, perhaps you could provide them to us."

As the nurse reached across the bed to hand a clipboard to Dana, Mallory began to mumble and move her head from side to side.

"Just a moment." Emily leaned over and put her ear close to Mallory's mouth.

"Please. We must go now," said the nurse. "In the meantime, we'd appreciate it if you'd fill out as much of this information as you can."

"Of course, we'll see what we can find. She carries those things in her wallet and her purse is missing."

"I understand," the nurse responded, as she followed the gurney holding the limp frail body out of the room.

"Let's wait in the cafeteria," suggested Emily.

"That sounds like a good idea," replied Detective Elliott. "I could use a coffee."

Walking down the hall with the women, he was relieved they'd found their friend, and she was alive. Now the investigation would have to determine what had happened to Mallory.

"Emily, could you make out anything Mallory was saying just before they took her out?" he asked.

"It was faint, but she kept repeating something that sounded like 'Pasqual, Pasqual'."

"I think that's a cookbook she has. The chef's name is Pasqual Sciarappa. I wonder why she would be thinking of that?" said Phebe.

Hearing the name Pasqual, the detective stopped and turned to them. "Ladies, do you have an address for Forrest Williams?"

CHAPTER 20

Later that evening, as they sat drinking coffee, Brad strolled into the cafeteria. Dana saw him first. "Brad, what are you doing here? I hope there's no problem."

"I saw an interesting news report last evening and called the detective in charge to see if they had identified the woman. Imagine my surprise when he told me it was your friend Mallory, and you were all at the hospital awaiting word on her condition. I was surprised when he told me my old friend, Dave Elliott, was with you."

"I knew I heard a familiar voice. How are you, Brad? Long time no see. Looks like you all know each other." Dave set a cup of coffee down for Dana and Phebe and a hot chocolate for Emily. Can I get you a coffee, Brad?"

"No thanks to the coffee and yes Dave, we met recently under unusual circumstances. That's a story for another time."

"Looks like the charge nurse is coming with information

for us," Phebe said, glancing toward the cafeteria entrance.

"Perfect timing, Brad. I'm glad you're here, I'd like to run something past you. Will you all excuse us for a little while?"

"Of course, Dave," said Phebe. "You know where Mallory's room is."

The three women turned their attention to the nurse.

"Ladies, your friend is back in her room and the staff is getting her settled in. She's in and out of consciousness. We expect the doctor to come in to speak to her if she's awake or to you, if she isn't."

The friends quietly entered Mallory's room and noticed her eyes were open, although she appeared groggy and was mumbling.

Drawn by the motion in the room as they approached the bed, Mallory glanced in their direction.

"Oh! I'm so glad to see you all. I know I'm in a hospital, but I don't know why. I have a terrible headache."

She said nothing about being assaulted or abducted.

Mallory's voice was raspy. "I remember, I needed to go to Forrest's ranch, but there was something else before that – something terrible." A tear ran down her cheek, finding its way to her puckered mouth as she held back a sob.

She didn't ask about her Lamborghini, so she must not know her purse, cell phone and ID, as well as her car, were missing.

In a calming voice Emily said, "Mallory, please don't worry. Just relax and rest now. That's the best thing. You're safe. I'm sure the police will get to the bottom of this soon. We'll fill you in on details as we know them."

A conversation near the door could be heard as a doctor, nurse and another member of the medical staff entered the room.

"Hello, Mallory. I'm Dr. Grafton. I will be overseeing your care. We have you hooked up to IVs and monitors to catch any sign of trouble as soon as possible. You were severely dehydrated when you came in. The IVs have saline solutions to rehydrate your system, broad spectrum antibiotics as a precautionary step and a mild pain medication for your headache. Physically, you're in reasonably good condition. Those bruises, although painful, will heal over time and I'll prescribe an antibiotic for those nasty cuts and abrasions. We've noticed you have memory issues, so I've ordered a CT scan. We'll see how you do after a good night's rest and expect to have more answers tomorrow.

"Your condition in the morning will determine the next steps to take. We're hopeful you'll be able to return home tomorrow evening or the next day, if there's someone to stay with you 24/7 for the next few days. Mallory, do you have any questions?"

Mallory had closed her eyes and again appeared to be asleep.

"Well, as I said, we'll revisit her condition in the morning. I'll be in to see her around 11:00 to 11:30. Will any of you be here?"

"We're going to take turns being with her throughout the night," said Phebe. "We'll make a point of all being available for your update tomorrow."

As the doctor and his team left the room, Detective Elliott and Brad entered.

"How's she doing? What did the doctor have to say?"

"Dr Grafton said she's in fairly good shape, physically. They're giving her fluids, antibiotics, and pain medication in the IVs. He said they'll know more tomorrow after she's rested. He's hopeful her memory issues will clear up over time."

Mallory opened her eyes and looked directly at Detective Elliott and Brad.

"Hi, Brad, I remember you, but who's your friend?"

"This is Detective Dave Elliott from the Palm Springs Police Department. He helped Phebe, Dana, and Emily with a missing persons report when they couldn't find you and he got them in to identify you."

In a weak voice Mallory managed to say, "Thank you, Detective. I'm sorry. I'm not good company. I'm so tired."

"Happy to help." He hesitated, then went on. "Mallory, Emily said you whispered something in her ear. She thinks it sounded like Pasqual. Do you remember saying something like that?"

Mallory's eyes brightened but dimmed again as she drifted off to sleep.

"Maybe she'll remember more tomorrow. Brad and I have a few things to get organized, so we'll be leaving now, but we'll be in touch tomorrow."

"Thank you so much for your help," the women said, as Brad and the detective left the room.

True to his word, Dr. Grafton arrived promptly at eleven the next morning.

"Good morning, Mallory. Oh, I see she's sleeping. As you all know, Mallory had a fitful start to the night and appeared to be having unpleasant dreams. We gave her a mild sleep medication that calmed her. I spoke with her during the night as she became more alert.

"Her physical health continues to improve, which is good news. I know you're all concerned with her memory lapses. I'm happy to report the CT scan shows no visible damage, although issues with memory rarely show up on brain scans. Her semantic memory appears intact, as she is aware of her personal history and can recall facts and common knowledge.

"Now episodic memory, simply put, is recollection of previous experiences in the context of time and place. A concussion most often presents as temporary amnesia and confusion. Keep in mind dramatic memory loss could also result from extreme emotional distress. This usually lasts a few hours, but could last days or weeks. Each patient is different. Rest is her friend."

Mallory opened her eyes. "Doctor, will my memories come back?"

"You did suffer a blow to the head, which accounts for your unconsciousness and your headache. However, I'm optimistic you'll have a full recovery once you're home and resting. Your memories may be intermittent, so it's a good idea to share them as they return. Don't hold them in.

"Since you have good friends willing to stay with you around the clock for a few days, how do you feel about going home this afternoon?"

"I would really like that, Doctor."

"I think that's best. I'll get the discharge started and you should be in your own home by dinner time. It was a pleasure meeting you, Mallory.

"Please call my office to schedule a follow up appointment within the next ten days."

CHAPTER 21

When they left the hospital, Detective Elliott contacted Arthur. He felt it was important the FBI and DEA hear what Arthur knew of Martine's connection to a nefarious Frenchman. The similarity of the names — Pascal, and Pasqual — connected to Martine and Mallory, was too close to be a coincidence. Dave felt certain Mallory hadn't been mumbling about a cookbook author.

While Dave was connecting with Arthur, Brad called his brother Chuck. It was time to share information and get Lance involved. After providing Lance with the current facts related to the investigation involving the women they had both met at the séance, it was agreed, both agencies were on the trail of the same criminal, Rene Pascal. Lance eagerly agreed to set up a meeting in the FBI conference room the next morning.

Those in attendance, along with Brad and Lance, included Lance's contact in Spain, as well as Brad's boss, both on conference call, Detective Elliott, and Arthur.

Introductions were made. Then Detective Elliott asked, "Arthur, can you tell the group what you previously told me about Martine and the Frenchman?"

"Yes, I'm so relieved this is coming to light." He sat down, rested his hands on his knees, wiped his eyes and cleared his throat.

"Marni – Martine -- and I enjoyed a long happy marriage. We shared confidences, but there were areas of her past she was uncomfortable discussing. She kept a diary that I read only after her death. I have it with me and will leave it if you feel it's necessary."

"Thank you. We'll safeguard it and return it to you as soon as possible. Please continue," said Brad.

" I knew her parents died when she and her older sister Nicole were young. Having no relatives to protect them, they grew up rough on the streets around the port of Marseilles. Nicole became a sought-after prostitute and earned enough to send Martine to a private school. She didn't want her sister to have the life she was living. Martine was sixteen, on school holiday and visiting Nicole, when one of Nicole's wealthy clients became obsessed with her and began stalking her.

"Nicole protected her by sending her to Los Angeles. She felt Martine would be safe in another country, far from Marseilles. This worked for a few years until Martine graduated from Cal Arts, where she'd earned a degree in art history. Her thesis topic addressed Middle Eastern antiquities.

"Walking off the stage with her diploma, Martine came face to face with the man who'd stalked her in Marseilles. He hooked his arm in hers and whispered in her ear. 'Keep quiet, *ma cherie,* and come with me. This is important. Your sister needs to see you'.

"The man then flew her to Mallorca in his private jet and held her captive for years, making escape impossible."

Arthur's voice cracked as he continued. "Although she was sexually abused and used in various illegal activities, Marni said he seemed most interested in her knowledge of antiquities.

"Always looking for a way out, she asked her abductor to send her to an art seminar at Stanford, addressing the theft of Middle Eastern antiquities. She convinced him the connections she would make, and the knowledge she would gain, would be invaluable to him.

"That's where we met and fell in love. I understand now that she was desperate to conceal herself from the Frenchman. But I know she loved me."

Arthur continued. "We married soon after we met and, along with changing her last name to Webster, she wanted her legal first name to be Marni. She cut her hair short and also changed the color. We were happy. We raised a family and lived here in Palm Springs after my retirement. Then something changed. She was on edge all the time. Finally, she confided that this horrible man had tracked her down. He insisted she smuggle something into Spain for him. I guess she'd done it before. She said he threatened to tell the police she was an international art thief. She was very anxious about Nicole's welfare but didn't know where she was or if she was even alive. Marni was scared and told him she wouldn't do it. He kept after her, terrorizing the last weeks of her life."

Arthur sighed, "I believe he's responsible for her death. She was active and vibrant with no health issues, always taking great care of herself. Within days of telling me this, she had what they called a heart attack. Just before she died, she was worried she'd told me too much. She was afraid the man would hurt me to get her to do what he wanted. I got the feeling she'd threatened to report him to the authorities. I'll never forget the name. She called him, 'Pascal'."

Arthur's information meshed with what the FBI and DEA had in their files. The name Mallory mumbled in the hospital seemed to connect her near-death experience to this same criminal. Critical questions remained. Law enforcement knew of Pascal, although he'd eluded the authorities for years. But who was Forrest and what was his connection to Pascal? Also, had Martine died of natural causes? Or was there something more sinister involved as her husband Arthur believed?

Arthur agreed to an exhumation if they felt it would reveal Marni's true cause of death.

The task force's mission was to incorporate every fact related to Pascal, including Mallory's information, as her abduction had occurred right after she met Pascal. When checking records for the date ranch, they found the title was held, not in Forrest's name, but in the name of an offshore corporation.

Rene Pascal had been on the radar of the DEA and FBI for years. The name, "Forrest Williams," had not shown up in any of the research on Pascal. Forrest, like a ghost, was on no one's radar.

It was agreed Brad and Lance would head up the task force. Detective Elliott and Chuck would be kept informed and would make themselves available, should the need arise. The group decided their next step would be for Brad to set up a meeting to find out what Mallory remembered about her trip to the date ranch.

Brad's call to Dana was answered with, "Hello Brad.

What's up?" She'd added a musical ring tone to his number, so she knew right away it was Brad.

Interesting, she knew it was me, he mused. "Dana, as you know, I work for the government. The DEA specifically. We've gathered information about some criminal activity and we'd like to interview Mallory. Has she been released from the hospital?"

"Yes, she's home, but she's really upset and has been crying a lot. I don't think she'd know anything about any illegal activities."

"We're just gathering facts at this point. Do you think she's up for a visit? Is her memory improving? We'd really like to hear more about her visit to the date ranch."

"I think that's a good idea. She's having flashbacks, so her memory is returning. Her conversation is all over the place, though. She's talking about cylinder seals and a mysterious man at Forrest's. Then she hesitates and starts crying."

"Do you think she's holding back?"

"I don't know."

"A visit from us may help. We'll be there shortly."

The security gate let out its now well-known squeal as Brad drove the Lincoln Town Car through.

They were met at the door by Phebe, who directed them to the large dining room table where Dana and Emily sat with Mallory, who wore her pajamas and robe, looking worried and pale.

"Mallory. Ladies. I'd like to introduce you to Lance. He's with the FBI. We're working together on an important case."

The women looked at Lance and then at each other.

"Oh my gosh! You look just like the college student

that was at the séance," exclaimed Emily.

"Yes. In fact that was me. I'm sorry to have deceived you all, but I was on company business that night and am not at liberty to explain further. I'm a bit older than a college student."

Mallory, though nervous, managed to smile at the young man's deception. Her memories had been flooding back and, although she thought of Dr. Grafton's advice to share them, she was tormented by the image of Toni's body lying for days without being found. She wasn't willing to talk about that yet. The stress was causing her sleeplessness, loss of appetite and a guilty conscience, not to mention the fear of what might happen to her.

"Brad and I would like to hear about your trip to the date ranch, Mallory. Do you think you're up to telling us about that?" asked Lance.

She paused, then quietly said, "I'll try."

"Mallory, just start wherever you'd like," said Brad.

"Okay." She took a deep breath and began. "It was dark. I couldn't find Monet."

Confused, Brad glanced at Dana who mouthed, "Her car."

"When lightning flashed, I spotted her far from where I'd left her. When I rushed over, I heard stones crunching behind me. Then I woke up in the hospital. That's all I remember. No, wait. I remember talking to Forrest. He was angry I said his painting was a fake."

"Was Forrest the only person there?" asked Brad.

"He said we were alone." Hesitating, she then continued. "But when I went to the bathroom, the light in the display case came on and an old man with a walking stick and a long scar on his face was standing right next to me. I was startled, but I'd seen other pieces of art that could bring me large commissions. I really need the money."

"Did this man talk to you?"

"Give me a minute. Yes, he said '*bonsoir*,' in a thick French accent, and told me the artifacts in the case were cylinder seals from Iraq. That's a big deal."

At the mention of cylinder seals, Lance raised his eyebrows and looked at Brad.

"Oh! Now I remember. Forrest introduced him as Pascal — Rene Pascal. That's exactly how he said it."

"Then, the old man said Toni told him all about me. I remember them wondering why Toni wasn't there."

"Can you remember any more about what happened before you went to find your car?"

"The old man, was putting on the charm. He said Toni suggested I take a trip to Mallorca for them. He and Forrest thought this was a great idea. Then they said something about a woman dying."

"Why did they want you to go to Mallorca?"

Mallory's speech slowed as she thought about this question. It seemed unreal even now.

"They wanted me to sell the cylinder seals. He said they knew I was desperate for money," she choked, "and this would solve all my problems."

"Did you agree?"

"I don't remember what I said. I just wanted to get out of there. Someone opened the door for me and I rushed out into the storm. Then I got hit on the head."

"Why did you go there, and why alone?"

"Oh, everything was so awful then, and Toni ..." She choked down a sob. "I'd seen Toni the night before."

The ringing of Mallory's phone interrupted what she was going to say about Toni.

Phebe jumped to her feet. "I'll answer that for you, Mallory. Hello. Crawford residence, Phebe speaking."

"Yes, Phebe. I remember you. This is Forrest Williams. I'd like to talk to Mallory."

Phebe pressed the phone to her chest, muffling the sound in the room. She whispered, "It's Forrest."

Mallory began to tremble as she looked from Brad to Lance.

Taking a notebook and pen from his shirt pocket, Brad scribbled the words: *Speak slowly, I'll help you.*

Shaking her head, she mouthed the words "No" and "Please."

"Just a moment, Forrest. I'll see if she feels well enough to talk. You may not be aware she's been in the hospital."

Lips quivering, Mallory slowly nodded her head in agreement with Brad's offer of help.

"Here she is, Forrest," said Phebe, as she handed the phone to Mallory.

Brad put his head next to Mallory's and tilted the phone so he could hear the conversation.

"Hello, Forrest."

"How are you, Mallory? I understand you were in the hospital."

"Yes, that's true. I'm still very weak and have an awful headache."

"Well Mallory, I don't want to rush you, but the matter of your trip is time sensitive. You'll love Mallorca. It's a beautiful place. Chopin wrote some of his best music there. Considering the first-class trip and the pay, I've no doubt you're anxious to go."

Brad wrote, *Stall. Call him back.*

"Forrest, I understand, but I'm exhausted. I'll have to call you back."

"I expect to hear from you by tomorrow. Oh, by the way, have you heard anything from Toni?"

"Toni?" she gasped. "No, I haven't heard from her. I'll call you back. Goodbye Forrest."

Brad noticed Mallory's hand was cold and damp as he took the phone from her.

"Mallory, how do you feel about going to Mallorca? You've been through quite an ordeal. Do you feel up to it?"

"No, I'm scared!"

"Lance and I, and others on the task force we've formed, are certain Pascal, and perhaps Forrest, are the bad actors we've been tracking for years. They're involved in unsavory, illegal, and inhumane acts spanning decades. This is as close as we've gotten to bringing Pascal to justice. In this strange turn of fate, you have his trust, and he needs your help."

Lance added, "Mallory, we know this is frightening and it could be dangerous. Like Brad said, we have experience planning this type of operation. So, if you feel up to it, we can prepare you. The agents involved are knowledgeable about keeping our operatives safe. Someone will be with you constantly. You'll never be alone."

"I trust you, but I need time to think about it and time to regain my strength."

Dana spoke up. "Brad, I think she's been through enough. Is it really wise for her to go alone? I mean, with no one she knows. I want to go with her."

"Yes, I agree," chimed in both Emily and Phebe. "We should all go."

Brad raised his eyebrows as he glanced at Lance, who said, "No. Definitely not. We can't put civilians at risk. We'll need all our resources to keep Mallory safe while tracking these two monsters."

They turned their attention to Mallory, as they heard her sniffle and begin to sob.

"Mallory, don't be afraid. We can take care of you, and you'll be helping to put some of the world's worst criminals in prison, where they belong."

"That's not it" Mallory choked. "You may want to arrest me rather than ask for my help. There's something else I need to tell you."

CHAPTER 22

Detective Elliott, along with Brad and Lance, found Toni's distinctive home near the mountains and entered through her front door, which was slightly ajar. Entering the foyer, they were hit with the pungent odor of decomposing flesh.

With the information Mallory had provided, the group proceeded through the living room and down the hall, to an adjoining office. Lying in a dried pool of blood next to a large desk lay Toni, with a long twisted purple scarf clutched in her right hand.

Detective Elliott made a call to summon the local medical examiner and crime scene investigation team, telling them the matter was urgent and involved the dead body of a local resident.

Careful not to disturb anything, the three put on gloves and booties.

"Did you notice the gash on her temple?" asked Lance.

"It tracks with the information Mallory provided when she said Toni lost her balance and fell into the straight edge of the desk. That part of the desk definitely has blood on it. And look! There's the purple scarf Mallory mentioned."

"Yes, it appears Mallory was telling the truth when she said this was an accident, but we can't make any assumptions. Let's see what the CSIs discover," cautioned Detective Elliott.

The coroner and CSIs arrived, further securing the crime scene. The coroner did an initial examination of the body as photographs were taken. The team then gently zipped the corpse into a black body bag and loaded it into the van for removal to the morgue.

"Detective?" CSI Carla was standing next to the desk holding a painting of purple lilacs. "This painting was conspicuously tilted. When I removed it, I found a safe built into the wall."

Elliott took note of the large safe on the wall where the painting had hung. "Interesting," he said. "I'll get our locksmith over here right away. Good catch, Carla!"

The locksmith arrived shortly and opened the safe, which contained stacks of cash, assorted jewelry, a few small art pieces, and a set of keys.

The photographer took photos of the safe's contents and the CSIs dusted for prints and swabbed surfaces for DNA. Once the evidence was secured in clear evidence bags, Carla spread the material out carefully on Toni's desk so the task force could do a cursory inspection.

"I wonder what these keys are for?" asked Elliott.

At that moment, Carla spoke up. "Maybe we can use them to open the desk drawers. They're all locked."

"Go ahead and try them," said the detective.

Carla found that one of the keys unlocked all of the

desk's drawers. Carefully opening them one at a time, she discovered a stack of three large unsealed envelopes in the middle drawer on the right. The photographer and CSI techs did an initial inspection and removed them. One was addressed to the DEA, another to CIA, and the last one to Interpol. Carla spoke up again, excited.

"Look what's underneath the envelopes!"

Brad and Dave approached and caught sight of an exotic-looking gold-plated pistol.

"This just gets more and more interesting," muttered Brad

"Brad, come over here and look at what's in the envelopes," said Lance. "It seems Toni's been building dossiers on some familiar people of interest."

Brad walked over to the desk and saw that the envelope contained folders labeled: Forrest Williams, Rene Pascal, Martine Duval and Mallory Crawford.

"My God! Does this get any weirder?" Brad exclaimed.

After a long pause, Elliott spoke. "This changes everything."

An hour later, Detective Elliott, Brad and Lance were back at Mallory's home. As before, Dana answered the door and invited them into the living room. After everyone was settled, Detective Elliott asked to speak to Mallory.

"I'm sorry," said Dana. "After you left, Mallory complained of a splitting headache and went to her room. She's exhausted. Today's events have come as quite a shock. We have to be careful because she's really fragile right now."

"I understand, but it's important we speak to her as soon as possible," replied the detective.

Dana stood, said she would check on Mallory and left

the room. Shortly, Mallory appeared, with Dana following close behind. She was still in her bedclothes, seemed utterly distraught and collapsed into a chair.

"Mallory," said Lance, "we just left Toni Vitale's home and the scene was generally as you described it, with one exception. We found evidence that implicates you as a person of interest in our investigation."

Mallory burst into tears. "Toni threatened to do something like this! But I promise you that I …"

Brad interrupted. "Stop, Mallory. Don't say another word. I advise you to get an attorney. You're going to need one."

CHAPTER 23

Forrest ranted impatiently as he paced the floor at the date ranch. "What the hell is wrong with that girl?" he roared. "She said she would call back with an answer. We can't wait around forever for her to get on board. I'm convinced she's in better shape than she's letting on."

When Mallory hadn't returned his call, Forrest grew more irritated with each passing hour. Last night he'd begun calling her and leaving phone messages.

"You assured me she was dependable." Pascal's raspy voice cut through the scene like a rusty knife. "What am I missing here?"

"She'll come around since she's desperate for cash."

"She'd be upset if she knew we weren't actually planning to pay her."

"That's beside the point. Once she's under our control, we can do whatever we want with her."

At that moment, the phone rang.

"Forrest. It's Mallory."

"It's about time. What took you so long?"

At Brad's suggestion, Mallory had spoken to her family attorney — a trusted college friend — who then spoke with the task force. They had worked out an agreement that would allow Mallory to assist Brad and Lance with their investigation. Though nervous, Mallory was now well-prepared for this conversation with Forrest and would accept his offer to courier the cylinder seals to Mallorca.

"Have you forgotten I'm recovering from a life-threatening attack and kidnapping?"

"How soon can you be ready? We need to get moving. We already have a buyer."

"There's a lot for me to consider. This is a big decision and I'm not feeling 100%. Are you assuming I'll accept the assignment? I won't be much good to you if I'm not fully recovered."

"What's holding you back? This'll be a big payday for you."

Brad was able to listen to this conversation, thanks to the DEA's state-of-the-art audio surveillance equipment he'd set up in Mallory's home.

He thought she was doing a great job, considering her emotional state. Mallory had a lot to process now that, in addition to everything else, she was a person of interest in the Toni Vitale investigation. He was glad she'd followed his advice to seek legal counsel and admired her willingness to cooperate. What she was about to undertake would require tremendous courage.

As he listened, Mallory continued. "Dr. Grafton says it may take a month for me to fully heal."

"A month? Unacceptable! I'll give you a week max," snapped Forrest. "First, you'll have to spend some time with Pascal and me so we can prepare you. We'll do it at your place."

"When?" she asked.

"We'll be there tomorrow afternoon … say around 2 o'clock."

Brad signaled to Mallory that she should accept and wrap up the call.

"I'll accept conditionally and see how my recovery goes, but I'm not promising anything."

"We'll make it easy for you, and don't forget the big payoff! We'll see you tomorrow," he barked, and abruptly ended the call.

"How does he know where I live?" Mallory whispered. Thinking that the two men might have been following her sent a chill down her spine.

Before Mallory's meeting the following day, Brad and Lance made a list of questions she should ask about her travel arrangements and courier role. They suggested she resist taking the assignment, so Forrest and Pascal would have to do a hard sell. Brad assured Mallory she would be perfectly safe during the meeting, as the two agents would be in the next room and would hear every word.

The next day, Forrest arrived alone at Mallory's home promptly at 2 pm, as promised. Phebe answered the door.

"Hi Forrest. Please come in. We met at your ranch a few days ago."

"Oh," Forrest grumbled, disappointed. "I didn't expect to see you. I was expecting to meet with Mallory alone."

"And Mallory was expecting you to show up with your business associate. I guess you were both wrong. Please follow me into the dining room and sit down. I'll get Mallory."

Phebe was concerned as she led her friend into the dining room. Mallory looked pale and was again wearing her bathrobe and slippers.

"May I get you some coffee or tea?" offered Phebe.

"Nothing for me," replied Forrest.

Forrest nodded a greeting to Mallory, then addressed Phebe directly. "You'll have to excuse us. We'll be making important business plans and want privacy."

"Of course," answered Phebe, leaving the dining room and closing the heavy wooden door.

"Forrest, I thought you said your partner would be with you."

"He's a busy man, Mallory. You have no idea what a big shot he is in international business. I can take care of everything that needs to be done." Forrest's gruff demeanor abruptly changed. His facial expression morphed into a big, friendly, insincere smile.

"Mallory, I'm afraid you and I may have gotten off on the wrong foot. Let's start again. As we've explained, Rene Pascal and I are in the business of acquiring and selling rare antiquities from the Middle East. You've seen some of our most valuable pieces. What we're asking you to do is simple and safe. We merely want you to deliver a small quantity of cylinder seals to a wealthy buyer at a luxury resort in Mallorca. That's where you'll be staying … in grand style, I might add."

"What's the name of the hotel? And why do you need me to deliver the seals? Couldn't you or one of your employees do it? Is there something fishy or even illegal about what you're doing?"

"You don't need to worry about any of those details. And no, there's nothing fishy; it's just a simple transaction among friends."

"Then why all the secrecy?"

"Isn't it obvious? The value of these seals is beyond imagining, so it's critical that our courier be discreet and above suspicion. With your knowledge of priceless art, travel experience and professional appearance, you're exactly what we need to complete this sale."

"I don't know," Mallory hesitated. "Something really seems off. And how much are you paying me?"

Forrest pulled a piece of paper and a pen from his pocket, wrote a number on it, and slid it across the table.

"That's a lot of money!"

"It's worth it to us. Say you'll do it." Forrest was practically salivating.

"Okay. I trust this is all above board and I really could use the cash."

"You won't regret it, Mallory. Imagine yourself lounging by the pool, sipping your favorite drink, looking out over the Mediterranean. Once you've delivered the goods, Mallorca will be your own special playground."

Forrest paused for a few moments, lost in his own thoughts. Then he got serious, making direct eye contact with Mallory. "I can't stress this enough. Rene and I insist on your complete discretion in this matter. You are to speak of it with no one — especially those friends who seem to be at your beck and call."

"Don't you think they'll wonder why I'm suddenly leaving town?"

"Tell them you deserve a vacation after all you've been through and you prefer going alone."

"I'm not sure they'll buy that," said Mallory. She knew her friends were already aware and that Phebe — along with Brad and Lance — were listening from another room.

Forrest continued with his sales pitch. "You'll fly with

us to Mallorca in Pascal's luxurious private jet."

"No way!" Mallory responded, suddenly frightened. "I'll feel much more comfortable traveling First Class on an international carrier like Iberia."

Forrest thought for a moment. *Pascal isn't going to like this change of plan. However, he's spoken many times about how his connections on Iberia help him move his art, drugs and prostitutes. I'm going to let her think she's won this one. She's more likely to trust us if we give her something.*

"All right. We can make that work."

"When will I be leaving?"

"Since the plan has changed and you're concerned about your health, we can push it a week, no more. For your own safety, you'll have less than twelve hours notice of your departure, so you should immediately locate your passport and gather your belongings.

"How will I get to the airport?"

"We'll send a limo for you."

Again, Mallory asked Forrest for information about where she'd be staying. Forrest reminded her of the confidential nature of selling the artifacts and keeping them safe from potential thieves. That's why information about her lodging had to remain private. However, as their meeting ended, he let it slip on his way out that the resort was on the island's north shore.

After Phebe shut the door behind Forrest, she, Brad and Lance joined Mallory in the dining room.

"Are you sure I can do this? How can you protect me if you don't know my flight and hotel information?"

Lance reminded Mallory of the combined agencies' vast resources and assured her she would be perfectly safe every step of the way.

Phebe saw Mallory back to bed and informed Brad and Lance she was going out for a bit. As she left the house, Brad and Lance sat down to discuss the next steps.

"Lance, let's have Elliott spend the night here and plant the tracking devices before that limo driver shows up."

Lance was quick to agree. Over the next few days, the two of them spent hours with Mallory getting her ready for the trip. They had to assume Forrest and Pascal were having her home watched, so they were careful with their comings and goings.

A different kind of preparation was taking place at Emily's home. With Mallory safe under the watchful eye of the task force, Phebe, Dana and Emily gathered to make their own plans.

Emily spoke first. "I don't care what Brad says, there's no way we're letting Mallory go through this alone."

"You're right, Emily. We're all in this together," said Dana.

Also," continued Emily, "I don't know how this figures in, but I'm the only one who's never been face-to-face with Forrest. He doesn't even know I exist. That could be useful as we go forward."

"That's right," said Dana. "We'll keep it in mind."

"So how will we travel to Mallorca without Mallory or Brad knowing?" asked Phebe.

"We know Mallory will be flying on Iberia out of LAX. Let's check out the most likely schedule."

Opening her laptop, Dana quickly identified the most promising flight options.

"Remember, Mallory will have about twelve hours notice of her departure," reminded Emily. "The three of us must be ready to leave at any moment."

Everyone paused to fully take in the seriousness of the situation.

"Let's investigate which resort is most promising on the north shore," said Dana. "We're likely to go through Customs in Madrid and then connect to Palma. That means we can go directly to the hotel after picking up our bags."

"We'll have more flexibility if we don't check any bags and rely on our carry-ons," added Phebe.

CHAPTER 24

Lance invited Brad to his office so they could make plans for Mallorca. Since they'd set up the task force after confirming they were after the same man and his criminal empire, it was urgent they work together to bring him down. Pascal's far-flung international organization encompassed the drug trade, artifact theft and sex trafficking.

Everything was moving along so quickly they hadn't had time to interact on a personal level. Brad was curious how someone so young could have reached the level Lance enjoyed with the FBI. "You seem young to have so much experience in the antiquities trade and you've built up quite a reputation within the Agency. What's your secret?"

"No secret, simply good genes. I've always looked younger than I am. I'll be forty-one my next birthday. This body has seen a lot of travel, dodged a few bullets, and recovered stolen art on every continent. I've spent time in Iraq and was there when the museum was ransacked."

"My God! Did you find any of the stolen cylinder seals?"

"I was posted to another part of the country and wasn't anywhere near the museum. However, my partner and I did retrieve a nice cache of cylinder seals from a private home in Iraq before they were smuggled out of the country."

"What an interesting career you've had."

"Yes, I've been fortunate to spend my life doing work I enjoy, while making the world a better place. I'm sure you feel the same."

"You're right, of course," said Brad. "So, let's talk about Rene Pascal. By combining the research done by our agencies, we've determined he leads one of the world's largest criminal cartels. He's got to be damned old by now and walks with a cane. We still have no idea when he was born. All we know is he was found on the docks of Marseille as a young child. Though self-educated, he's very smart and quickly made a name for himself in the criminal world. His age must be slowing him down. Strange as it seems, he was legitimately contracted by the US military to transport basic supplies for the troops in Iraq. Knowing all this, he's still a ghost to us."

Lance added, "We've learned Williams and Vitale were in Iraq at the same time and on Pascal's payroll. We know where Forrest is but have no evidence connecting him to Pascal's illegal activities. The information we retrieved at Toni Vitale's home is interesting, but is it credible? Unfortunately, she won't be answering any questions. First and foremost, I'm after Rene Pascal. I've chased him all over the world. He's one slippery fish. I'm thrilled we have a chance to capture him on his home turf. I don't know how the Spanish government could allow that piece of slime to settle in their country."

"Bribery is a well-established practice in Spain and can make anything possible," Brad sighed. "We've also located a well-fortified palacio in Mallorca. It's name, 'The Fortress,' is incorporated under the same legal entity as the date ranch. It's near the Formentor Lighthouse, northeast of Pollenca. I've never been to Spain," he continued, "but I'm fluent in Spanish. My work often took me to Mexico, and I've rounded up more than a few drug lords. I would love to cut off the snake's head so we could rid ourselves of Pascal's criminal influence."

Lance added, "The FBI was unaware of Williams until Pascal's visit to the date ranch. Perhaps they're planning a change of command. Williams is younger than Pascal and is able to travel more easily. We're closer to ending this than we've ever been. I can't believe Mallory's involved with such lowlifes."

"Neither can I. Though I've known her for just a brief time it seems unlikely she's capable of doing the things laid out in the Vitale file and a murderer. Unfortunately, it's going to be an uphill battle for her to clear herself. Helping us will go a long way in her favor. I don't think we should travel on the same plane with her. We could enlist a female agent to befriend her on the plane. When they land in Mallorca, she could just grab a cab to wherever they house Mallory."

"That'll work, Brad. You and I can take an FBI plane to Madrid or Seville, and then helicopter up to Puig Major. That's the highest peak, where the American radar station is located on Mallorca."

"That makes sense," Brad responded. "They'll likely

put her up in a five-star resort; there are only a couple on the north shore. Don't most Spanish resorts have private cottages that aren't connected to the main hotel?"

"Yes, they call those cottages 'villas.' Pascal probably already has one reserved for Mallory. He'll want a secluded setting for her to conduct his business.

"Dave Elliott will put tracking devices in her luggage. I believe one should be in her purse and another in her suitcase. Maybe one of our agencies will spring for an expensive large bag with a hidden compartment."

Brad was happy they were crafting a workable plan. "My experience tells me they won't, and no doubt Pascal will want control over her luggage for his own reasons. But we'll still have time to place the trackers."

"We should get to Mallorca long before they do. Lance, has your boss talked to Interpol yet?"

"Absolutely, they're in constant contact. Seems some big shot from one of the Middle Eastern countries is planning to fly to Palma to see Pascal. I don't know where the information came from, but I'll bet it's accurate."

"I'll be glad when we have Pascal and Forrest in custody and this caper is over. Even though we told Mallory's friends to steer clear, I'm afraid they're going to try something."

"Oh, good lord. I hope not! They do seem determined to protect her. Should we speak with them again to warn them off?"

"I'll take care of it," said Brad. "Can you think of anything we haven't covered, Lance? It'll take me less than an hour to prepare my travel pack."

"That about covers it for now. My boss will tell me if there have been any updates from Interpol and I'll arrange for the female agent to fly with Mallory."

"Let's meet at the Jockey Club in DC, say day after to-morrow at 7 p.m. We can finalize our plans over a nice dinner."

CHAPTER 25

The intercom buzzed in the residence.

"Yes?"

"Your limo to the airport, madame."

It was dark as Mallory stepped around her oversized Louis Vuitton rolling luggage, which Forrest had sent over yesterday. He'd emphasized the need to exhibit a wealthy demeanor and instructed her to pack her most expensive clothing and jewelry.

Ceni had enjoyed lavishing her with designer clothing and jewels during their marriage, so this was not a problem. Ready cash was the problem. She understood the airline had a weight limit, but Forrest told her she need not be concerned with minor technicalities.

Looking through the peephole, she saw a hulking man, well over six feet, with bulging muscles that could not be hidden by his chauffeur's jacket.

She unlocked and opened the door.

"Good morning, madame." He saluted with two fingers touching the bill of his cap. "Is this your only bag?" he asked in a French accent, as he reached in and lifted the luggage as if it weighed mere ounces.

It was difficult to determine his expression. Framing his ruddy complexion was a wiry beard. Although neatly trimmed, it hid most of his face and was tucked into his collar.

"Yes, just that and the tote bag that contains my gate opener, purse, passport and a few essentials for the flight."

"Let's get started then."

As she slid her arms into her faux fur jacket, he handed her a thick manila envelope. It was sealed. The man hadn't introduced himself and she wasn't going to ask. What she didn't know was safest.

Striding ahead of her, he secured her luggage in the back of the black stretch SUV and was ready with the rear door open when she reached him.

"This will be an uneventful trip to LAX, madame. Please relax and enjoy the ride."

A cool breeze tossed her hair as she bent to enter the limo. Sliding across the back seat, Mallory noticed a Louis Vuitton makeup case in grey graphite with its distinctive blue stripe and MC monogram that matched the suitcase Forrest had sent.

"Yes, that is your bag. However, you have no need to concern yourself with it. I will manage it for you along with your other luggage. Should you find it in your way, let me know and I will move it further across the seat. No need for you to touch it."

Although it was comfortable inside the limo, her body was shaking; not with cold, but with nervous apprehension. Never had she imagined her life taking such a turn.

When Ceni was alive she was so happy, and there was no reason to expect that to change.

Sliding her cold hands into her coat pocket, she realized she was still holding the thick envelope. Opening the sealed flap, she removed its contents. She counted $2,000 in US currency and €1,800 in euros, each in various denominations. A folio from Iberia contained her roundtrip airline tickets, a reservation confirmation for ten days at the Encanto, and a letter certifying travel insurance for 30 days. Nice name, Encanto, meaning charming or glamour. *Well, we will see,* thought Mallory. Was Forrest acting in her best interests with the insurance because of her recent medical issues? Or did he have an ulterior motive? Hopefully, this would be something she wouldn't need, but she had to admit it did give her comfort. A 3"x5" white index card slid out from the documents and landed on her lap. In a nearly illegible scrawl, it informed her: We thought you might like to stay and relax after your assignment is complete. Please consider this a holiday.

It all seemed surreal to her. Everything had come together so quickly. She really didn't want to go to Mallorca to sell the cylinder seals. Regardless of what the FBI or local police might charge her with regarding Toni's allegations against her, or even worse, Toni's death, she knew for sure what she was about to do was illegal on an international scale. She was so afraid of Forrest and Pascal, she hadn't been able to keep anything down, except her old standby, Cream of Wheat.

Leaving Palm Springs behind, the limo moved smoothly along Highway 111 and easily maneuvered the curve to merge with traffic on Interstate 10. Few vehicles were on the road this early, but she knew as they approached LA, it could be a nightmare.

She really might enjoy free time in Mallorca, but not alone. Lance was adamant Emily, Phebe and Dana were, under no circumstances, to be anywhere near this operation. It was just too dangerous and would complicate things. He and Brad were relieved when her friends had agreed, but she saw the glint in Phebe's eye. She knew her friends were determined and independent. They hadn't made it this far in life by following orders.

The brightly lit highway darkened as the limo moved to the left to enter the Badlands area of the 60 freeway. Badlands was exactly what the area reminded her of. The two narrow lanes curved one way and then the other with a steep drop-off on either side. Mallory braced herself in the corner of the seat, pressing her feet against the floorboard. The elevation changed as the limo made its way through the dark and desolate area. She knew there had been fatal accidents here and never drove it alone. She couldn't see anything through the windows until suddenly, a tractor trailer rig pulled in front of the limo, causing the chauffeur to tap the brakes and blurt out, "Idiot!"

The freeway lit up again as they neared the end of the Badlands, and Mallory could see the white diamond shapes painted on the lanes to her left, as the limo eased into the carpool lane. Her body was shaking and although she feared Forrest and Pascal and what she was committed to doing for them and the FBI, she closed her eyes and prayed they would soon arrive at LAX.

She felt the limo slow and bright lights stream across her eyelids, as she realized she must have dozed off out of sheer exhaustion. Cautiously she opened her eyes and realized two hours had passed since the Badlands scare.

When they pulled up curbside to the International Bradley Terminal, true to his word, the chauffeur took her baggage from the rear of the limo and reached in to grab the makeup case.

"Please wait a moment, madame. I'll take care of your bags and escort you through check-in."

Looking out the window, she saw the chauffeur approach a tall thin man wearing the uniform of Iberia Airlines. They shook hands and exchanged envelopes. The employee tucked his into the inside pocket of his jacket and then walked off with both her suitcase and the makeup case.

Mallory took this opportunity to snap a picture of her itinerary and other documents and send them to Dana. She immediately deleted this text from her phone. No matter what happened, someone would know where she was.

The chauffeur opened the door just as Mallory dropped the phone into her purse. "Please follow me, Ms. Crawford. Here is your first-class boarding pass and entry to the executive lounge. As I said, I'll help you through check-in and escort you to the lounge. You'll be boarding in about one hour."

He held out his hand and added, "I'll be needing your phone. It will be returned later."

Mallory reluctantly handed him the phone and dutifully followed him to the TSA entrance, where she showed her passport and boarding pass. The chauffeur then presented his identification, and both were passed through. This was strange. Mallory hadn't seen him present a passport or boarding pass.

They had no need for the people mover, as a golf cart met them and whisked them away to the international lounge.

"Madame, your first-class boarding will be soon. It was a pleasure assisting you." He again saluted her with two fingers to the bill of his cap. As he strode away, she noticed he passed under an overhead sign that read To Private Terminals.

CHAPTER 26

Bernard felt Mallory watching him as he left her and walked down the private plane concourse. He removed his chauffeur's jacket and hat and, with a swift movement, placed them over his arm, the hat tucked in so it wouldn't fall. He found Pascal's plane, a small white jet with green markings on the tail.

Although a normal jet of this size could hold up to fourteen passengers, Pascal had the inside reconfigured to transport his specific cargo while accommodating four reclining passenger seats and a couch, which currently held Forrest. He was covering all his contingencies. Bernard had become his trusted bodyguard, pilot and all round factotum. Pascal knew how fortunate he was to have Bernard in his employ, but he would never tell him. Looking into the cockpit, Bernard saw his boss slouched in the copilot's seat and recognized the smoky smell of scotch whiskey.

"You'd like me to drive, wouldn't you?"

"*Merci*, Bernard. I'll just stay here and sleep. Let's get going."

"Rene, I need to check out the plane first and file a flight plan. I also need to see if we have sufficient fuel."

Pascal had already passed out.

Bernard checked the galley and found no food, no water, nothing. And it looked like Rene had cleaned out the scotch bin. He sure doesn't like to follow the rules. *Mon Dieu!*

Bernard proceeded to perform the necessary preflight check. He also asked Forrest if he would like to go with him to the pilot's lounge where he could inquire about food and water. "I need to file our flight plan. We don't want to cross the pond without someone knowing our whereabouts. It's a big ocean and we are a little plane."

"I think I'll just relax here on this couch. Will it be long before we leave?"

Bernard shrugged his shoulders, left the plane, and strode over to the pilot's lounge. It was a spacious room with comfortable chairs and a large table where pilots could use their computers to check maps to determine their flight plans. As Bernard surveyed the room, he saw no food; not even a refrigerator. He addressed a man wearing an airport jacket who stood behind a counter at the back of the room. "Don't you have any snack machines or water? I'm flying to Spain."

"Sorry sir, all I can give you is a couple bottles of water and some candy bars. I suggest you go back up the concourse to Starbucks and McDonald's to buy food and coffee. Our catering truck won't be back until late tonight or tomorrow. I'm sure you know you'll need a layover to refuel before you fly across the Atlantic."

'This is the first time I've been to LAX."

"Then welcome!" The attendant smiled.

"Can you suggest an airport where I could get catering to bring food on board?"

"If I were you, I'd make Burlington, Vermont my first stop. It's a small, but international airport where it's easy to get in and out quickly. I can't say the same for any of the other airports near or on a coastline. I could call catering for you and have food waiting when you land."

"Much appreciated."

"I'll need your credit card for the fuel, sir."

Bernard pulled out his wallet and handed over his personal VISA card. He realized the card was issued in France and he'd be charged a currency conversion fee, but it wouldn't matter; Rene would reimburse him. Logging into the flight app on his cell phone, he checked the map and filed his flight plan. Before he returned to the plane, he walked back up the concourse straight to Starbucks, bought a case of water, a half dozen bagels, cream cheese, and a Starbucks Coffee Traveler filled with dark roast. He asked the store manager for someone to help him take everything back to the plane, but not before he stopped at the McDonald's stall for burgers and fries. *That should get us to Burlington.*

After giving the young man $10 for bringing the food on board, before he even sat down, Bernard scarfed down two hamburgers and a fistful of fries, along with a large cup of coffee.

Feeling he could now last for a few hours without collapsing from starvation, he stuffed two bottles of water in the pocket at the side of the pilot's seat. Satisfied with what he had done, Bernard looked over at Rene, who was dead to the world, mouth agape. Then he checked on Forrest who was also sleeping. Grabbing another hamburger and a sleeve of fries, he made himself comfortable in the pilot's seat. He donned his glasses, checked the controls, and requested instructions for takeoff from the tower. Within minutes, his flight was cleared. Unusual for an airport of this size. *From what I hear, it generally takes at least thirty minutes to get off the ground. I feel lucky.*

Hours later, Pascal's thunderous snoring was interrupted as Bernard radioed the Burlington tower for landing instructions.

"What the hell, Bernard? he snorted. Where are we? Why are you landing?"

"We need provisions and fuel. I can't fly without food in my stomach. The flight deck at LAX told me this was a great airport for a quick landing and takeoff, so here we are. It will take a short time to refuel and for catering to bring food on board."

"You take care of it, Bernard. I'm going back to sleep."

I'm glad I'm driving. Rene would have us in the ocean upside down. It's sure much easier flying than driving that limo.

It was an uneventful flight to Mallorca, where they all exited the plane. Bernard left the two men and strolled into the main terminal to meet Mallory's flight.

Pascal and Forrest crossed the tarmac to Pascal's helicopter, climbed aboard, and flew to his fortress, high on a promontory overlooking the sea. Pascal wanted to confirm the arrival time of his buyer from the Middle East and check that Nicole was still under his control.

CHAPTER 27

In all chaos there is a cosmos, in all disorder a secret order.
— Carl Jung

Describing an island paradise while speaking of chaos and disorder may seem paradoxical. The setting is Mallorca, a place of stunning beauty located in the Mediterranean Sea due east of Valencia, Spain.

A man stands on a rugged cliff gazing out at turquoise blue waters. A honeymooning couple hikes through lush green foliage to picnic in a secluded cove. A mother and daughter shop in a picturesque country market. A class of high school students are guided through the magnificent Le Seu Cathedral, which took over four hundred years to build. The island literally bursts with artisan, cultural and culinary delights. If one's tastes are drawn to a vibrant party scene, a Mallorcan club can entice even the most reclusive traveler with its music and dancing.

Mallorca has for centuries been a magnet for people seeking relaxation and escape, having attracted the likes of composer, Frédéric Chopin, author George Sand and even surrealist artist, Joan Miró. More recently Princess Diana and Mick Jagger have graced its shores. In short, Mallorca — and its ancient capital, Palma — offers a wide array of options for personal pleasure.

It was into this Eden-like place that several groups of visitors arrived in Palma almost simultaneously: not to enjoy the island's riches, but to conduct business. An undercurrent of evil was about to taint this blissful scene.

Lance and Brad were first to arrive. They came by helicopter to Puig Major, a US radar site found in the Serra de Tramuntana Mountain range on the northeast part of the island. Here they were provided with a four-wheel drive SUV and given directions to Palma. There they would meet with their FBI and Interpol counterparts to complete their plan to finally capture Rene Pascal and destroy his criminal enterprise.

Pascal and Forrest Williams had landed at a private terminal at Palma International Airport, where they were whisked away by helicopter to Pascal's luxurious villa on the northeast shore. Bernard remained behind to meet Mallory's flight and drive her to a secluded villa.

Hours later, an Iberia jet unloaded five more passengers of interest.

First to deplane was an anxious Mallory, who had agreed with Pascal to deliver the cylinder seals to his buyer. He was unaware she was secretly working with a combined FBI-DEA-Interpol task force.

Next to disembark were Mallory's three friends — Emily, Phebe and Dana — who were there to protect her. Phebe had traveled alone dressed as an aging hippie from the late 1960s. She wore a long gray wig, loose, unfashionable clothing and Birkenstock sandals. Emily and Dana had sat together in economy class dressed in nuns' habits. All three had successfully escaped Mallory's notice on the flight. There was also a single female passenger, Nina Mireles, an FBI agent recruited by Lance, to befriend Mallory on the flight and ease her fears. Unbeknownst to her handlers, there was much more to know about Nina.

Soon, another private jet landed nearby, carrying a wealthy middle eastern gentleman — a well-known collector of art and antiquities. He was in Mallorca to buy a priceless collection of cylinder seals from Rene Pascal. Imagine his astonishment to be met by authorities and taken immediately to FBI headquarters, arrested and interrogated for hours. Eventually he made a deal and spilled all the information he had on Pascal's business, including the fact that he had never met with him before face to face. This new information inspired the task force to hatch a plan to substitute an Arabic-speaking agent for the buyer and carry out the assignment to get to Pascal.

It may seem that these numerous comings and goings added chaos to Mallorca's tranquil, serene setting. But remember Carl Jung's wise words, "In all chaos there is a cosmos, in all disorder a secret order."

CHAPTER 28

Entering the terminal in Mallorca, Mallory was surprised to see the chauffeur who had driven her to LAX holding a sign with bold print proclaiming, Crawford. With his cool demeanor, he greeted her and returned her phone. "It is a pleasure to serve you again, madame. I'll take you to your limo."

Since she hadn't previously asked his name, she thought it advantageous to do so now. "We haven't actually been introduced. You know my name, but I don't know yours."

"Bernard, madame. My name is Bernard. Please follow me. Your luggage, of course, has been taken care of."

How could he be so efficient?

Arriving at the resort, she felt a pleasant wisp of salt on her tongue from the ocean breeze. Under any other circumstances she would've been thrilled with this experience. Did Forrest really think she would stay after she completed her assignment?

Bernard escorted her through the spacious lobby. Sparkling floor to ceiling glass doors folded open to reveal the edge of a cliff and the sound of thundering ocean waves crashing below.

"Hola," Bernard addressed the woman at the VIP reception desk. "You are expecting Ms. Crawford, I believe?"

"Of course. Welcome, Ms. Crawford. It's my pleasure to serve you." The smiling blonde woman, with an American accent and sparkling hazel eyes, continued. "You have been entered on our roll. You'll find your luggage awaits you in your residence. Please place your index finger on the scanner. This will transfer your print to your entry door and will also avail you of all the resort's most upscale facilities. Complimentary, of course. I'm sure you'll enjoy your stay. My name is Olivia. Here's my card. Contact me any time, day or night, for any reason. I'm at your service."

As Bernard walked with her along a path lined with a riot of low-lying multicolored flowers and tall trees swaying in the breeze, Mallory noticed a well-built man talking into the cuff of his white shirt. Realizing he was hotel security, she became aware of others like him scattered along the path.

Taking notice of the heavily carved wooden entry door, Mallory recognized Poseidon, god of the sea, being fed grapes by his consort, Amphitrite. She had seen these Greek gods before depicted in various art works.

Bernard waited while Mallory pressed her finger against the bronze pad discreetly placed near the oversized door handle. Hearing an electronic click, he then said, "Monsieur Pascal will contact you tomorrow." Touching two fingers to the bill of his cap, he turned away and walked back the way they had come.

As she entered, she saw the monogrammed Louis Vuitton makeup case sitting prominently on the entry table. The case had followed her every move, without her having touched it once.

The villa was a two-bedroom standalone building with a beautiful bath, decorated with tiles in ocean hues. The bathroom ceiling displayed water nymphs cavorting in the sea. She and Ceni had traveled much of the world but had never been to Spain. As luxurious as this place was, it could not distract from the very real and dangerous reason she was here.

Since she couldn't stop shaking, Mallory rubbed her hands together rapidly to warm them. From experience, she knew this signaled the onset of an anxiety attack.

Reaching into her purse, she pulled out a bottle of Ativan. Her doctor had prescribed it to calm her nerves after Ceni's death. She'd kept the unused pills, and brought them to Mallorca, as she felt they could be helpful during this frightening time. Popping one in her mouth, she swallowed — no water needed.

After arranging her clothing in the wardrobe and toiletries in the bathroom, she lay on the bed and pulled a Caribbean blue chenille throw over her for warmth. Closing her eyes, hoping for relief from the stress of recent events, she instead felt her chest tightening with fear. *What will happen when I return home, assuming I make it through the next few days?* Forcing this unnerving thought from her mind, she purposely concentrated on her recent plane trip, which had been a luxury she'd never experienced before.

Forrest had said she was not to worry about cost. She had no idea he and Pascal were so wealthy, but there certainly was a fortune somewhere.

Practicing her deep breathing exercise, she became lost in the memories of her recent flight.

From the moment she'd entered the spacious cabin, the relaxing music, ambient lighting, and muted sound of a waterfall had calmed her. The first-class suite reserved for her, one of only fourteen, was on the plane's upper deck. She recalled closing the privacy screen and reclining the seat to a full flat bed. The calming burble of the waterfall provided a sense of well-being and allowed her to sleep for a couple of hours.

Upon waking, she'd admired the well-appointed space, which included a vanity table with drawers and an illuminated mirror, a personal wardrobe, dining table and private mini bar.

Despite these luxuries, she'd become restless and longed for friendly social interaction. She recalled being tempted by the area reserved for first and business class passengers, because it had a cocktail lounge with its own bartender, comfortable seating, and most of all, promised a bit of normalcy. Conversation with those who knew nothing of her circumstance was appealing.

As she had entered the softly lit bar, she'd been pleased to see well-dressed travelers, content in conversation, enjoying cocktails and appetizers. Taking a seat on a plush swivel chair with its own side table, she'd ordered a dry martini — Chopin, with a garlic stuffed olive. After taking a sip, she leaned back, sighed, and closed her eyes.

"Hello. Sorry to bother you, but it looks like we're the only two here traveling alone."

Squinting her eyes, Mallory had seen a matronly woman with an out-of-date pixie haircut addressing her. Settling herself in the seat opposite Mallory, she remarked, "Mind if I join you?"

Suddenly, her daydream of the luxurious flight was interrupted by the repeated ringing of a nearby phone. Opening her eyes, she realized she was lying on the luxurious bed at the Encanto. She rolled to her right and saw the blinking light of the phone on the night table alerting her to an incoming call.

"Hello?"

"Hi Mallory, this is Nina Mireles. Remember me? We met on the plane. Isn't this a wonderful resort? My room is on the top floor and is simply divine! How about meeting me at the main pool? We can get a bite to eat and something to drink."

Now fully awake, she considered the invitation. No one had said she had to remain in her villa, and she did appreciate the distraction the woman had provided during the flight. "Sure, Nina. Give me ten minutes."

CHAPTER 29

Sit down and shut up!" Lance's shouted demand was un-characteristic, since he was known by his colleagues for being cool under pressure and utterly unflappable.

An angry little man took a seat and said nothing. Since his arrest a few hours earlier, he'd been unleashing a steady stream of invective. More annoying, the barrage of insults was in Arabic. An FBI translator had been summoned and would be available to assist Lance and Brad in the inter-rogation.

The sparsely furnished, windowless room was claustro-phobic. The air was heavy and damp and there was no air conditioning. Designed to arouse discomfort and fear, it contained only a metal table and three folding chairs.

The man was physically unremarkable; about 5'5", 150 pounds, with an olive complexion that could've been Lati-no, Italian, or middle-eastern. Wearing a pricey Brioni suit, a crisp white Dior dress shirt, an understated Hermès silk tie and shiny black leather oxfords, he was dressed to impress. According to his passport, his name was Habib, but according to the task force, he'd also had numerous aliases over the years.

When the translator, Joe Mustafa, arrived, Brad gave up his seat, stood near the back wall and looked menacing. Lance took the lead and wasted no time getting down to business.

"Good afternoon," he began politely. "Your name, sir?

Mr. Habib avoided the interrogator's face and looked at the wall. More silence. The translator made the request to him in Arabic, but received no response.

Lance slammed his fist on the table separating the two men. With the unexpected loud noise, Habib began to shake.

"We know everything about you, Mr. Habib, because we've been following you for some time. We know you speak perfect English, having been educated at Oxford. Our translator is just for show. That mirror behind you is two-way. Agents from the FBI, DEA and Interpol are listening and watching your every move. We have solid evidence proving you've been receiving stolen art and antiquities for decades. With that documentation, you'll be powerless to avoid a prison cell for the rest of your life."

"I have rights! I demand to be taken to the Saudi embassy in Madrid! Immediately!" Mr. Habib had miraculously recovered his fluency in English.

"We've already been in touch with the Saudi ambassador and he assures us we can keep you as long as we like. I'm afraid your goose is cooked, my friend," snapped Lance.

As the interrogation continued, Mr. Habib realized the gravity of his situation and refused to answer any further questions. After a long silence, Lance abruptly stood, gestured to Brad and Joe to follow, and walked toward the door to confer with his law enforcement colleagues.

"Wait! Where are you going? It's hot in here and I have to take a piss!"

"You should've thought of that before," said Lance, walking out and slamming the door behind him.

"He's terrified," said Lance, turning to Joe Mustafa.

Mustafa was a grandson of Kuwaiti immigrants. He'd been born and raised in Brooklyn and was American through and through. An experienced FBI agent in the Antiquities Division, Joe had worked with Lance before. He was conversant in many languages, including Arabic. To the casual observer, he bore a striking resemblance to Habib. It was for this reason — not his translating skills — that he had been brought into the interrogation room.

"Let's let him sweat for a couple of hours," said Lance. "By then he'll be ready to do anything to make a deal and give up information on Pascal."

When the three men finally re-entered the room, Brad stood next to the door while Lance and Joe took seats across the table from Habib. Perspiration ran down Habib's face and neck, staining his already soaked designer shirt. The acrid smell of urine hung in the air.

"Please!" Habib implored. "I've wet myself!"

"We can help you, to be sure," replied Lance, "but you need to help us too."

"I'll do anything!" said Habib.

Brad escorted him to a men's room down the hall. Habib entered a stall and turned to close the door.

"Leave it open," Brad said.

Habib relieved himself, then walked to the wash basin, where he used wet paper towels to wipe his face and neck and made a fruitless attempt to remove the urine from his slacks. After handing him a water bottle, Brad brought him back into the interrogation room. The questioning continued, and this time, Habib folded like a cheap deck of cards. One fact was of particular interest. Neither Pascal nor Forrest had ever seen Habib in person.

"We know you'll be meeting Pascal tomorrow to buy a collection of cylinder seals, stolen from the Iraq Museum in Baghdad. What can you tell us about that meeting?"

CHAPTER 30

Mallory checked the resort map to find the shortest route to the main pool. It was halfway around the complex and thankfully nowhere near the equestrian area. She really wasn't in the mood for the smell of horses. Slipping on her sandals and plopping a wide-brimmed scrunchy hat on her head, she opened the door to bright sunlight and a warm breeze. In the distance she could hear seagulls squawking and ocean waves breaking against the shore. Mallory pulled the hat down further, nearly covered her face, as she slowly walked toward the pool.

Although she passed four security guards, none made eye contact with her. *Why do they need so many guards? Is the King of England staying here? Or perhaps a rock star?*

Reaching the pool, she used the sensor to open the gate and immediately gained access, just as Olivia had promised.

The entire length of the Olympic-sized pool sported an

infinity edge nestled along the cliffside, giving the impression that if you swam in that direction, you'd be floating in the never-ending ocean.

She saw a group of women, including a curly-haired girl of about five years and a trim, grey-haired woman who appeared to be in her eighties. Mallory assumed the woman was the matriarch of the group and the child's grandmother. As the girl brushed her grandmother's hair, it was interesting to see the women were amazingly comfortable with themselves, each other, and their bodies. All were bare-breasted and wearing various swim bottoms from blousy to nearly nonexistent. While not part of this group, there were two burly male specimens, wearing neon thong Speedos, who were trying to push each other into the deep end of the pool.

The visual curiosities continued as two nuns in full habits came through the gate with what looked like an aging hippie in tow. Having been the product of a Catholic girl's school, Mallory recalled the sing-song voices of the girls as they chanted in unison: "The headdress is called the veil and is the outer fabric covering. The quaff is the close-fitting white cap that holds the headdress in place. The wimple is the white piece that covers the neck and cheeks. Never, ever touch the nun's habit."

Mallory knew from experience the headdress made it impossible to glance at the face of a nun unless directly in front of her. The nuns, heads down, strolled along the pool deck.

Engrossed in the tableau, she nearly missed Nina waving from an aqua blue cabana nestled in the far corner closest to the pool bar. Potted palms provided extra shade to the cabana.

"Hi, Mallory. Are you enjoying your holiday? They

sure named this resort right when they chose 'Encanto.' It really is charming and glamorous. No doubt you have experience with the lifestyle. I noticed you were chauffeured in a private limo at Palma airport. How luxurious!" Pinching her nose she continued, "I, on the other hand, shared a taxi with a rotund man with questionable hygiene."

"It was actually an unusual luxury." Mallory laughed. "Not soon to be repeated."

"You mentioned on the flight that you're an art dealer. Do you have a big sale here in Mallorca?"

"Something like that."

"Well, I personally am here to relax, relax, relax," Nina said, as she sat in one of the red padded lounge chairs. "My latest client gave me this trip as a bonus for my work. I jumped at the opportunity and here I am." She wiped the corners of her mouth with the thumb and first finger of her left hand then, sighing, reclined her lounge. "I'm going to visit galleries, but I'm really looking forward to touring the Formentor Lighthouse. I'm drawn to historic architecture and the lighthouse was built in 1863. It also feeds into my sense of adventure. It's the highest lighthouse in the western Mediterranean Sea, located high on a cliff at the northernmost point of the island. It's only about seven miles up a beautiful, paved road."

Mallory, only half listening as she spread an oversized towel across her lounge commented, "That sounds wonderfully peaceful."

"Well, yes and no. It's in a rugged and isolated spot. The drive is beautiful, if a bit precarious, and scary in spots. Because the road is hilly and narrow with switchbacks and drop-offs to the sea, it's often closed to private cars. Much of the time you can only get there by walking, bicycling or taking a tour bus."

A tall, trim young man approached from the bar and asked if he could get them drinks or food.

"Absolutely, thank you, I'll have a double Old Fashioned on the rocks, short glass," Nina responded.

"Dry martini, Chopin vodka with a garlic stuffed olive, please," chimed in Mallory.

As the server turned toward the bar, Nina piped in. "Oh! And munchies too, please."

"Coming right up," replied the server.

Returning her attention to Mallory, Nina asked, "This really is a great resort, but what's with all the security?"

"I agree and was wondering if the King of England was staying. It does seem a bit excessive for such a quiet resort."

Deciding to be the questioner rather than the questioned, Mallory asked, "What do you do for a living, Nina?"

"Oh, I'm an independent consultant. I do a little of this and a little of that. It's very boring work, but it does take me all over the globe. Not an easy accomplishment for someone our age. Sorry, I meant my age. No doubt I have a few years on you."

"Not necessarily, Nina. I'm feeling older by the day. Although this is a glorious location, I'll be relieved to return home." She caught her breath as the guilt of Toni's death unexpectedly overcame her.

"Why are you so uptight, Mallory?"

Her question was left unanswered as the wandering nuns approached; heads bent in prayer. A warm breeze caused the skirt of one to brush against the canvas of the cabana.

Ever the good Catholic, Mallory addressed them. "Hello sisters. I pray you're enjoying your afternoon." She knew only priests took confession, but she thought she might feel less stressed if she could talk to these nuns. "Could you spare time for me? I'd like your spiritual advice."

"Certainly, my dear," one of the nuns raised her head as she addressed Mallory. "Whenever you're ready, you may join us in our stroll and talk at your leisure."

Mallory noticeably straightened her posture, her mouth gaping, as she made eye contact with the nun. *Oh my God! These aren't nuns, and this is no hippie. The nuns are Dana and Emily, and the hippie is Phebe.*

Not wanting Nina to question why she looked shocked at seeing a nun, Mallory turned fully toward the nuns, giving Nina her back.

"I'm ready right now." Speaking over her shoulder, she addressed her new companion. "Nina, do you mind? I won't be long."

"No, go ahead," Nina replied as she leaned back on her lounge, put her feet up, covered her head with a hat and put on her mirrored sunglasses. "I'll just take a cat nap."

"What in the hell are you doing here? Nuns and an old hippie! I can't believe it. Well, yes, I guess I can. You know Brad and Lance were emphatic that you come nowhere near this operation. It's too dangerous and you could complicate their plans!"

"Hang on," said Dana. "We can talk, but first Emily and Phebe should step away. My 'spiritual advice' should appear to be personal to you alone."

"You're right," agreed Phebe, taking full advantage of her flower child appearance and tossing a long mane of hair. She gently took Emily's arm and guided them slowly away, allowing Mallory and Dana privacy as they advanced toward the opposite end of the pool deck.

The thunder of crashing waves against the shoreline

below punctuated the conversation, as Dana emphatically informed Mallory. "You had to know there was no way we'd let you undertake this situation without us. Regardless of what anyone thinks, we won't be letting you out of our sight. If all goes well, great. But there's a very real chance that things could go sideways, and you could face great danger. In that case, we will do whatever we feel is necessary. No more discussion. Case closed, Mallory."

Glancing through the mirrored lenses of her oversized sunglasses, Nina was curious as she observed the animated conversation between Mallory and the nun. *What's that about?* she wondered.

CHAPTER 31

Mallory's heart skipped a beat when she realized the nuns and the hippie strolling around the pool were her friends. Knowing her most trusted friends were close helped reduce the anxiety she had been feeling. Mallory gathered her belongings from the pool chair and said goodbye to Nina. Walking back to her villa, she noticed the same security guards patrolling the area and wondered if they were there to protect the guests or the property. At this time of day, her villa was shaded by gigantic trees, turning it into what could have been a perfect spot for a romantic rendezvous under different circumstances.

Mallory was glad she wouldn't have the seals much longer. She still felt uneasy, even though Brad and Lance had assured her they would be nearby to protect her from Pascal and his cronies. Pushing open the heavy carved door, she flicked on the light and was stunned at the sight confronting her. Pascal and Forrest were sitting in two large chairs, enjoying drinks from her bar. She didn't know what to say.

"Hello Mallory," Pascal greeted her. He continued talking before Mallory could say anything. "We want to make certain you had a good flight. You'll be meeting our buyer tomorrow. We'd like to do it here in your villa."

Mallory was aghast to find these men in her private space. She had to sit down before she collapsed. Looking at them, she made a weak reply. "How did you get in here?"

"It wasn't difficult. I have contacts everywhere. We saw you at the pool with two nuns. What was that about? We also noticed you've met our associate, Nina Mireles."

"What do you mean, 'our associate'? I met Nina on the plane."

"That meeting was no accident."

When Mallory heard Pascal's comments, she hesitated. Absorbing what he'd just said, it took all her energy to remain composed. Finally she said, "I don't want the meeting here. I'd be more comfortable in a public place, like the dining room or the pool area."

"I'm running this operation, in case you've forgotten." Pascal paused for a moment and then decided. "The pool area will work," he said, thinking it could be to his advantage. Abruptly changing the subject, he then observed, "We checked and saw the makeup case is still locked. You're smart not to have messed with it."

Taken aback by the conversation and at the thought they were so easily able to enter her villa, Mallory was scared. Her voice quivering, she asked, "You said the pool area but didn't say what time. Will they be giving me cash?"

"Four o'clock, and no, you won't be getting any money. Everything will be managed by wire transfer."

Adding to the conversation, Forrest sounded irritated as he informed her, "Mallory, none of this is your concern. You just show up at the pool at four tomorrow with the makeup case."

"Right now, I'm just tired and confused," Mallory murmured quietly. "You told me this would be easy and safe. Now I'm not so sure. All I know is, I want this to be over as soon as possible so I can go back to my quiet life in Palm Springs."

Forrest knew Pascal planned to keep Mallory under his control until she agreed to continue working for him. She was a great replacement for Martine; smart, well-educated, and knowledgeable about fine art and antiquities. He also knew Pascal would force her if she didn't cooperate.

"Would you two mind leaving, so I can have a little rest? I've agreed to meet Nina for dinner." Mallory was afraid of saying anything else that might anger them.

Several moments passed before Pascal rose from his chair and motioned Forrest to do the same. They silently left the villa. When the door closed behind them, Mallory let out a huge sigh of relief and collapsed in the chair. She closed her eyes for what seemed like a few seconds, only to discover more than an hour had passed.

She sat, contemplating the day's events when the doorbell rang.

"Mallory?"

She recognized Brad's voice and, after looking through the peep hole, opened the door. Brad stood on the threshold with Lance at his side.

Mallory ushered them in. "You missed Pascal and Forrest. They left about an hour ago."

"We know. We've been watching and saw them enter

your villa while you were at the pool. We recognized Forrest and now know what Pascal looks like. Are you all right? We hear you're having dinner with our associate, Nina Mireles."

As much as Mallory wanted to hide the stunned look on her face, she was afraid she had blown it. Agent Mireles, Associate Mireles. *Holy shit! She's playing both sides of the field!*

"I'm okay. I meet the buyer at four tomorrow at the pool."

Lance informed her, "You'll be handing over the seals to our guy, Mustafa. They'll be calling him Habib. We've already arrested and detained Mr. Habib, the real buyer. Pascal will want to stay out of sight but will undoubtedly have a trusted colleague there to manage the transaction and protect his interests."

"That will most likely be Forrest, since he seems to be involved in everything so far." Mallory took a deep breath, then said "I'm really uncomfortable about doing this."

"Don't worry, Mallory. I know this is happening at a fast clip. The entire resort will be overseen by agents from Interpol, FBI, DEA, and local police. You'll be completely safe."

"I wish I had your confidence. I'm getting more white-knuckled with every passing moment."

"You'll be fine," said Brad. "We've got you covered."

"Just get me out of here in one piece, and safely home to Palm Springs."

Mallory's body was shivering. Without a word, she abruptly walked to the sliding doors leading to her private deck. With her back to the two men, she began to hyperventilate as she looked out to sea. She was clearly terrified and unsteady on her feet.

"Is something else bothering you, Mallory?" asked Brad.

"You might say that. Pascal says Nina works for him."

CHAPTER 32

It was 4 o'clock in the afternoon when everything finally came together.

Quiet for a busy resort, there were relatively few people enjoying the main pool area. Even vacationers observed the tradition of "siesta," so many were in their rooms sleeping off their busy morning pursuits, heavy lunches and exotic drinks. Those who were present seemed to be engaging in solitary interests, like reading, floating in the pool or getting full body massages in private poolside cabanas. No one could have predicted what happened next.

The cast of characters was interesting and diverse. All three of Mallory's friends, heavily disguised, appeared to be relaxing near the pool. Emily and Dana in their nuns' habits chatted quietly at a round table under a brightly colored umbrella. Phebe, shrouded in her retro hippie garb, lay reading on a shaded lounge near the pool's cliffside.

Lance and Brad were either standing or on the move,

paying close attention to everyone present. Careful in their movements, neither wished to attract attention. Dressed as tourists, they blended easily into the scene. Encanto's security team, highly visible on the pathways, was represented here by one man, who stood unobtrusively off to the side.

Forrest Williams, clad in shorts, a tee shirt, sunglasses and a straw hat, sipped a cerveza while planting himself at the outdoor bar between the far end of the pool and the cliff.

After a sleepless night, Mallory had spent a quiet day in her villa, dreading the meet with Pascal's buyer. Knowing the man was actually an FBI agent did not ease her nerves. Since yesterday, she'd had no further contact with either the task force or Pascal.

Her dinner with Nina the previous night had been awkward and they'd spent the time making small talk. Mercifully, they'd cut their evening short and both had retired early.

At ten minutes to four, there was a knock on Mallory's door. After checking the peep hole, she identified the visitor as Bernard, as expected. Opening the door, she beckoned him inside.

"Let's go," he said. "Madame, you'll be carrying the makeup case."

Mallory picked up the case and followed Bernard out the door and up the path to the main pool. The shaded path wound through a lush cluster of native bushes, bougainvillea, plumeria and fan palms. Once inside the pool area, Bernard led her to a small table near the shallow end and asked her to sit while he brought the buyer from the lobby.

When Bernard left, a nervous Mallory checked her surroundings. She could see Lance standing near the pool's entrance. Bernard had walked right past him with no sign of recognition, underscoring the fact they'd never seen each other before. She could also see Brad retrieving a red beach ball from the pool for a small boy playing nearby. A security guard was in conversation with the bartender. Although comforted knowing Phebe, Dana and Emily were also close, she was still concerned they'd put themselves in danger on her account.

Bernard reentered the pool area escorting a small, slim man immaculately dressed in an expensive suit. This must be Lance's guy, Mustafa. He really looks the part, although out of place for the setting. The two made their way to Mallory's table.

"This is Mr. Pascal's associate, Mallory Crawford," said Bernard. "Please sit down. May I offer you a drink? Coffee? Tea? Something stronger?"

"No. Let's do business."

Visibly agitated after sitting down, the little man scowled and tapped his feet nervously. He turned and spoke to Bernard in Arabic.

"Who is this woman and why is she here? I expected to be dealing directly with Pascal. Something's not right. Are we being recorded? Are you with the police?" He stood up to leave.

"No, no, Mr. Habib," responded Bernard in Arabic. "Please relax."

"No. You relax. I will not deal with a woman. If I can't meet with Pascal, the deal is off."

"Sir. One moment, please. I promise you we'll resolve this to your satisfaction. Please excuse me while I make a quick call."

Bernard stepped away, leaving Habib sitting with his back to a speechless Mallory. As he pulled out his phone to call Pascal, he heard the ding of an arriving text. It was from Forrest.

```
I've been listening and texted the boss.
Take Habib and Mallory to the boat. He
wants to do the deal at the Fortress.
```

At that moment, a piercing scream interrupted the tranquil scene and a distraught woman ran breathlessly toward the security guard.

"Help! It's my little boy," she cried. "He must have gone after that beach ball again. He's lying on the bottom of the pool right there." She pointed toward the deep end. "Please help! I can't swim."

A loud splash signaled that someone had already dived into the pool to rescue the boy. Mallory noted with admiration that the someone was none other than Brad. The child was the same one he'd helped just minutes ago. Curious about what was happening, guests scurried to the pool's edge. While Emily stood with the boy's mother to offer support, Dana knelt, peering into the water.

"Look," she shouted. "He's being brought up by that man!" Getting a closer look, she instantly recognized Brad. There was a big "whoosh" as the boy was hoisted out of the water and handed up to the security guard, who immediately began performing CPR. Everything happened in seconds. Brad's muscles flexed as he pulled himself out of the pool and suddenly found himself face to face with a nun. *Jesus, it's Dana! What the hell is she doing here? And what's that outfit she's wearing?*

Fortunately, the two had the good sense to keep silent

and gave no sign they knew each other. Brad thought, *If Dana's here, then Emily and Phebe must not be far behind.*

Dana stood and shouted to the gathering crowd, "Is there a doctor or nurse here?"

Taking advantage of the chaos, Bernard directed Mallory and Habib to follow him away from the pool, toward the cliff.

"Let's get out of here," he said and pointed to a gate in the fence at the edge of the cliff. "Come with me."

Habib was clearly rattled by this new turn of events. "What's going on? I don't want to be part of this."

Bernard reassured him by saying, "I'm taking you to Pascal. Just follow my lead and everything will work out. Mallory, grab the case and give it to Forrest."

The activity at the pool was focused entirely on saving the child's life. No one was paying attention to Bernard, Habib or Mallory.

Law enforcement had anticipated Pascal would be present at the transaction and prepared accordingly. They had planned to arrest him the moment the exchange was complete, remove him from the pool area and take him out through the lobby to a waiting van for transport to Palma. Although aware of the locked gate, they knew it led to a perilous descent to the ocean below. For this reason they had eliminated it as a possible escape route.

As the three moved toward the cliff, Forrest joined them from the bar, taking the case from Mallory. They walked so close to Phebe that Bernard accidentally knocked off her big straw hat. Forrest took one look and instantly recognized the woman he'd met just weeks before at his date ranch and again at Mallory's home. Without missing a beat, he grabbed her roughly by the arm and said, "You're coming with me! Now!"

Approaching the cliff's edge, they saw a padlocked gate with a posted sign.

Peligro!
No entre.

Having previously checked out this escape route, Bernard had known he might have to deal with the lock and was prepared. Without hesitation, he removed a small hammer from his jacket and, in seconds, was able to bump the lock open.

As the gate creaked open, Mallory stood still. "Doesn't peligro mean danger?" she worried aloud.

"We're all going to be fine. Just be careful and keep moving," Bernard responded.

The path down the rocky face was narrow and treacherous, leading to a small cove. It was so dangerous that resort guests weren't permitted to use it. The group of five, with Bernard leading, worked their way down the rocky trail single file, trying hard not to stumble. Hoping to calm Habib, Bernard tried to take his arm to help him past a few sharp outcroppings, but he resisted, preferring to manage on his own. Forrest, on the other hand, pushed Phebe and Mallory ahead to move quickly, despite the danger. No one spoke.

CHAPTER 33

As they made their way down the dangerous path, Bernard realized he'd become hyper observant. He wasn't sure why, but thought it had something to do with the man he'd passed on his way to meet Habib. Bernard had seen him several times around the resort alone and once with another man — the same man who'd jumped into the pool to save the kid. They didn't appear to be any more than acquaintances; certainly not traveling companions or a couple. The guy didn't look relaxed enough to be on holiday and he seemed a little too interested when Habib had raised his voice earlier.

When Forrest grabbed the arm of the hippie and pushed her through the gate, Bernard noticed she made eye contact with Mallory just a little too long. Who was she and what did Forrest know that he didn't? *What's going on here?* wondered Bernard.

"Mr. Habib, please let me take your arm. I see you

slipping on the rocks, and it would be a painful fall. Just plant your feet carefully and don't look down or up. Look straight ahead."

"What's going on, and who are all these people? This is not what I expected!" Then Habib, suddenly distracted by a helicopter, looked up. Sunlight shimmering off the waves caused him to squint and momentarily lose his balance. "Yes, I believe I will take your arm."

Making their way around a switchback, another startling sight greeted them. Floating on the low surf below was a state-of-the-art, candy apple red boat.

"What an amazing cigarette boat!" exclaimed Habib.

The undercover agent was familiar with cigarette boats and knew they were so coveted by criminals that drug cartels had gained control of the manufacturer and now churned them out themselves, built to their exact specifications. This was a huge blow to law enforcement, until the precision engineered go-fast boat was developed specifically to combat smuggling of goods and humans.

"It surely is," said Bernard. "It's been my pleasure to be the helmsman of that beauty."

They reached the dock ahead of Forrest, who was still in control of Mallory and the ragged-looking woman, who had now lost her wig.

Forrest shouted, "Bernard, get Mr. Habib on board. He'll be taking the seat up front, next to Mr. Pascal. The women will sit in the rear."

"That is my intention."

As they boarded, an elderly man stood. Gripping the back of one of the front seats, he addressed Forrest. "Bernard will take the wheel for this trip." Noticing the extra passenger, he added "Who is that woman and why is she here?"

"She's a friend of Mallory's. I don't know why she's here, but I will find out."

Satisfied for now, Pascal turned his attention to the little man standing near him. "Good afternoon, Mr. Habib. I am Rene Pascal. I have been anxious to meet you." He offered his hand to the undercover agent.

"Yes, as I told your man, it is fitting that I deal only with you personally." Shaking Pascal's hand he added, "A man's business is a man's business."

Feeling relaxed after his night at the Fortress, Pascal smiled. "I totally agree and welcome you aboard the Rum Runner. She's a beauty, my sexiest woman. A forty-one foot carbon edition, exceedingly rare. And a smooth ride. She'll take us home in no time. We have much to talk about. From here on you will have a luxurious, enjoyable visit. We'll get the business details out of the way and then celebrate with a nice gold rum from Jamaica. You do enjoy rum?"

"Yes, thank you, I surely do. I am anxious to complete our business, but perhaps a slight reprieve from the excitement is called for." Concerned at the unexpected turn of events and now being without law enforcement protection, Mustafa — aka Habib — played his part, not knowing how this operation had gone sideways so fast.

"We'll be on our way then. The trip will be fast and exhilarating. The most powerful waves at Cala Major can reach over six feet but are not expected for a few hours – a mere nothing for my Rum Runner. Bernard, take the pilot's seat. *Vite vite!* Mr. Habib, the carbon roof panel and wind screen will protect you from the wind and sea spray. You can be comfortable while I entertain you with the history of this boat and how she came to me."

Forrest, ignored during this conversation, grudgingly

stepped to the rear of the boat. "You two sit on the outside," he instructed Mallory and Phebe. "I'll take the center seat. Don't say a word."

Dark clouds began forming in the distance as Bernard revved the engines and the boat rapidly moved away from shore. Phebe, eyes wide, clutched at the voluminous clothing twisting about her body while Mallory, pale with fear, sat, hands clutched in her lap, her hair blowing wildly about her head.

The roar of the Rum Runner's powerful engines reached Encanto's pool area just as a doctor took charge of the small boy.

Brad grabbed a towel from a nearby lounge and wiped it over his face and through his hair. He looked around, expecting to see Mallory and Habib in the curious crowd. They weren't there. However, two nuns were. They stood, shoulders touching, and holding hands. Brad had recognized Dana as he brought the boy to the surface, but made a point of not reacting. Now with no doubt about their identity, he growled, "You two stay right where you are!"

Turning to Lance he asked, "Where the hell could they have gone? Did they enter the hotel?"

"I was concerned with the boy and looked away for just seconds. Damn!" he swore as he pulled the phone from his shorts pocket. Cupping it in his hands, he punched the keypad and spoke. In less than a minute he shoved the phone back into his shorts and said, "The Interpol guys in the van say no one passed them. They also said they've seen this before and they always have a backup boat and helicopter at the ready."

"Brad," Lance continued, "maybe they did manage to get to a boat." He pointed to a gate in the fence. "I see the lock is lying on the ground."

"Do you think they took Mallory and Habib down the cliff?"

"Sure, looks that way," Lance responded. "And that's a pretty powerful engine taking off. The Interpol agents said they've seen similar situations. Let's see how they've handled them."

"We have something else to deal with first. It won't take long. Take a look at those nuns."

"Don't tell me! We were specific. We ordered them not to follow Mallory to Mallorca."

"That's right Lance, but evidently they don't take orders well."

Lance, red-faced, joined Brad as he approached Dana and Emily. "If you two can listen this time, we'll connect with you after we've located Mallory. She's now in grave danger and the two of you have only complicated the situation. I assume you're staying at the Encanto. Do you think you can stay in your room until we come for you? It may be some time." He paused, making eye contact with Dana and Emily, and then spoke emphatically. "I mean in your room! Nowhere else."

Dana embarrassed, looked down at her feet as Emily said, "Yes, we'll do as you ask, but it's not only Mallory who's in danger now. We saw Forrest grab Phebe," she said pointing to the open gate. "He forced her through that gate with Mallory and two other men."

"What were you thinking? Not one of the three of you have the common sense of …"

"Not now, Lance. We'll take care of this later. Let's get to the van. We've got our work cut out for us. You two, please go to your room, where you'll at least be safe and out of our way."

After meeting with the Interpol agents, Brad and Lance were driven to Encanto's marina, where they boarded a high-speed boat with Guardia Civil prominently displayed on its side. Dive equipment was visibly stored aboard; weapons were hidden below.

"Isn't this pretty obvious?" Brad asked.

"Not to worry," answered one of the agents. "We run these boats constantly. Our air surveillance team informed us that a boat picked up passengers at the base of the cliff and headed to a well-fortified private encampment that has been on our watchlist for years. We have no actionable information, but we persist, and they're used to seeing our patrols."

Lance added, "As a member of the FBI Art Crime Team, I've been on similar cases, although never in Spain, and never with civilians involved. We'll need to develop a plan on the fly."

While the Guardia Civil speedboat was leaving the dock, the cigarette boat, with its peculiar mix of occupants, slowed as it approached what looked like, an impenetrable rock wall. Bernard moved the control lever forward to reverse the engines, causing the boat to quietly float toward the sheer cliff face, as raindrops speckled the wind screen.

Phebe could see a red light flashing as Bernard aimed a device at the cliff face and the rock wall opened out as though fitted with steel French doors.

The cigarette boat with its passengers, slipped inside onto a boat lift and the huge doors closed.

CHAPTER 34

The graying sky and the howl of the wind were shut out as the boat and its passengers were pulled into a cavernous space and up to a boat dock. As her eyes adjusted, Phebe became anxious in this unknown dungeon-like environment, although she was relieved to be sheltered inside and glad to be getting off the boat. Neither she nor Mallory had been protected from the sea spray and light rain that pelted them as the boat raced across the gulf between the Encanto and the Fortress. Phebe scanned her surroundings, desperately looking for escape routes. None were apparent.

To manage her stress, she concentrated on the cables that had taken control of the boat. As a child, Phebe had seen her grandparents' boat moored like this. She remembered watching their boat attach itself to cable runners. Her grandfather would push a button that enabled the boat to move steadily up the ramp to their back door. This was the same type of mechanism, only stronger and more sophisticated.

A low groan brought her attention to Mallory. As Phebe leaned forward to see around Forrest, she felt the mounting terror and lingering effects of her recent kidnapping were overwhelming Mallory, as she appeared paler by the moment. Forrest gave her a quick sideways glance but made no move to help her.

Everyone stayed seated until they came to a complete stop. Then Bernard reached up to a handrail to pull himself from the boat. The back of his jacket rose as he did so, revealing a gun tucked into the waistband of his trousers. Pulling his jacket down, he turned and extended a hand to Pascal and then Habib, helping them off the boat.

Glancing over his shoulder, Pascal directed, "Forrest, take the women up to the service area and stay with them. Nicole will be there, and she'll know what to do." Forrest reluctantly agreed, though he was tired of being ordered around like a servant.

Their steps echoed as the men crossed the concrete platform to a wide steel door. Bernard entered a code into the keypad and shouldered the door open. Knowing Forrest did not have the combination, he left the door ajar.

Pascal led the man he knew as Habib through the steel door across what looked like an unfurnished waiting room, to an elevator. "Mr. Habib, you are one of only a handful of people to enter my private home. I know you will appreciate all you see." He leaned against the wall of the elevator as they ascended.

"Thank you. I'm very much looking forward to your hospitality." Having seen a well-armed Bernard exit the boat, he felt naked without his own weapon.

Arriving at the main floor of the Fortress, the elevator doors silently opened. Stepping out, Pascal again spoke to Habib. "Please follow me to the library, where we will enjoy The Last Drop, a 1976 Jamaican rum. Don't worry, it's not my last drop. I have a case of the stuff. We can relax and do business without interruption. When we're finished, we will see what entertainment we can find."

Habib nodded a quiet thank you. As he followed Pascal, he was stunned by the opulence surrounding him. The large foyer felt even more spacious with wide staircases on either side curving up twenty-five feet, where they joined to form a landing. Unbelievable! His eyes moved to paintings hung nearly touching on the walls. *Oh my God! The treasures in this room could fill a museum gallery. There are masterpieces by Klimt, da Vinci, Renoir, Van Gogh, and more modern masters like Miró, Dali and even Picasso.* Habib — aka Mustafa — knew that despite the best efforts of the Monuments Men after WWII, there were still nearly 100,000 unrecovered items that had been stolen by the Nazis. *These were no doubt some of them. It will be a great day for the antiquities division if we recover all this, the cylinder seals and arrest Pascal too.*

Back at the boat, Forrest, feeling slighted by not being invited to join the men, nudged Mallory's hip with his foot. She didn't move. Her eyes were closed, and she'd slumped down in her seat. He thought she might have fainted.

"Get your dirty feet off her," Phebe growled. "Can't you see she's ill?" Phebe worried Mallory might be relapsing from her ordeal in Joshua Tree and felt sure there would be no medical help here.

"Mallory, you can't stay in the boat. Get out now."

Forrest raised his voice impatiently, trying to wake her.

"Let me help." Phebe reached for Mallory, but Forrest pushed her away.

"She doesn't need you." He was rapidly losing his temper.

Phebe saw her friend had passed out. Forrest realized that as well, and yanked Mallory to her feet facing him. He squatted down, threw her over his shoulder like a sack of potatoes, stood, and stepped out of the boat. "Let's go!" he shouted at Phebe.

Shocked by the ease with which Forrest manhandled Mallory, Phebe bit her tongue and pulled herself out of the boat. She rushed to join him as he approached the steel door. They took the elevator to a large service and storage area one floor up. Not trusting him with Mallory and fearing his temper, Phebe stayed close to Forrest.

When the elevator doors opened, Phebe and Forrest, who still carried Mallory, found themselves in a spacious, but poorly lit room filled with cabinets and storage racks. Unopened boxes of all sizes lined the walls, and a large bronze sculpture graced each side of the elevator doors. When her eyes became accustomed to the darkness, Phebe checked out the space, looking for anything — anything that might help her deal with this horrific situation. In an arched doorway to her left, she noticed an elegant woman — in her fifties — standing as still as the bronze statues.

"Nicole," said Forrest. "Pascal says you'll know what to do with these women."

As the woman approached, her extraordinarily beautiful clothing and jewelry belied the worn expression on her face and the dullness of her turquoise eyes.

"Of course. Please follow me, *s'il vous plait*," she answered in a thick French accent, leading them back into the elevator. "They can join me in my quarters." When all were inside, she pressed a button for the fourth floor.

Who is this woman? wondered Phebe. *And what is she doing here?*

There was much the friends from Palm Springs were unaware of, and when that information was revealed, it would change everything.

Although Brad and Lance had not met this woman, they knew much of her history. This was Nicole, the sister of Arthur Webster's late wife. Arthur had told them his wife, Marni, and her older sister Nicole, orphaned as children, grew up on the dangerous streets of Marseilles. Desperate for money, Nicole had prostituted herself for their survival. When she was just a teenager, a man named Pascal had taken control of her life.

Pascal told Nicole that if she stayed with him, her sister would be safe. Should Nicole abandon him, Martine would die.

Over the years, the women had secretly communicated through various trusted sources. This arrangement was agonizing for them both, but necessary, given the situation. Nicole was content in the knowledge that her sister was finally a happy, fulfilled wife and mother, practicing her art, and living in a picturesque desert town in California.

A couple of years ago, Nicole had received her last cryptic message from Martine, smuggled in at great risk by private courier. It read:

```
He's here and wants me to work for him
again. I refuse. Don't worry. Miss you.
Love.
```

This carefully worded message had caused Nicole

many sleepless nights. She worried about Martine and hoped she was okay. Pascal had been to Mallorca often but had made no mention of her sister. She was terrified to broach the subject with him. Today's arrival of Pascal with his trusted bodyguard and Forrest with the two American women, was shocking, but offered Nicole an opportunity. Maybe, just maybe, she could find out something about her sister.

When the elevator stopped and the doors opened, the group entered a broad corridor and walked some distance to a huge wooden door on the right. Walking inside, Phebe instantly became aware that she was in the most luxurious sleeping quarters she'd ever seen, worthy of a queen.

The wooden ceiling was high and elaborately detailed with carved ocean scenes at each corner and a shimmering crystal chandelier hanging from the center. Prominent in the middle of the room was a canopied bed that looked as if it could accommodate half a dozen people. Arranged on richly woven oriental rugs, the sitting area contained an oversized sofa, an eight-foot coffee table and two large, padded chairs. White Carrera marble reaching to the ceiling and surrounding the fireplace, gave the sitting area an illusion of safety. Beautiful damask drapes framed the windows, and the glass French doors revealed an ornate balcony and the coming storm beyond.

Recessed into the wall, opposite the marble fireplace, a narrow door with a snake carved into its dark wood looked out of place and ominous among this opulence. It remained closed, not revealing its purpose.

Forrest grunted and carelessly dumped Mallory on the bed. Without a word, he turned and left, locking the door behind him.

To hell with Pascal's orders to stay with the women. He clenched his jaw in anger. *I won't be dismissed again. We're partners, aren't we?*

"Oh shit, how do we get out now?" Phebe's stomach roiled. She felt she had no control over this situation. Rushing to the narrow wooden door, she thought might be an exit, Phebe heard the woman exclaim "Stop! Don't open it!"

It was too late. Phebe recoiled in horror. Looking into the dimly lit space, she saw a sleeping cot pushed against a stone wall. The small dungeon-like space also featured steel bars and heavy chains attached to the walls. The woman approached and quietly shut the door."You'll find no way out there," she continued. "Who are you and why has Pascal brought you here?"

"I'm Phebe and my friend is Mallory. We've been kid-napped. How in the hell do we get out now that the door is locked, and who are you?" She began wringing her hands.

"My name is Nicole; I have been a captive here for years. *Mon dieu!* Pascal says I am the love of his life, and he is taking care of me. He is mean and dangerous. I've only seen the man called Forrest twice before. He also is not kind."

Although her English was heavily accented, Phebe could understand her.

Phebe asked herself, *Can I trust her? We're in a hell of a mess. Where are Lance and Brad? I wish I knew what to do.*

Regaining consciousness, Mallory moved her right arm to cover her eyes. When Nicole saw her moving and heard her moaning, she hurried to the bathroom, brought back a warm wet washcloth and towels, and began gently wiping the sweat from Mallory's face.

"Where am I? What's going on?"

"You are in my sleeping quarters at the Fortress, Rene

Pascal's private residence," said Nicole.

"You fainted when we were on the boat," added Phebe. "Forrest carried you up here and left you on the bed. Mallory, this is Nicole. She lives here."

"You're Americans? Why did Pascal bring you here?"

"It's a long story. We met Pascal and Forrest in California — in Palm Springs. Forrest hired Mallory to do an art appraisal for him and I went with her to his date ranch. The art was fake. A lot has happened since then. Mallory brought stolen antiquities for him to a buyer here in Mallorca. She had no choice, but …"

"You're from Palm Springs?" Nicole interrupted. "My sister Martine lives there. Do you know her? She too was once a courier — carried things for him."

CHAPTER 35

Pascal's private library offered visitors a glimpse into how the man saw himself. Having grown up from nothing, he had aspired to greatness from an early age. Thus, his beloved Fortress — arguably the grandest property in Mallorca — served as a constant reminder to the billionaires and world leaders who vacationed there, that Rene Pascal was someone to be reckoned with, respected and even envied. While he was rumored to be a criminal, nothing had ever been proven, so who he was remained a mystery to most people.

The library was a large, circular turret room, 25 feet in diameter and 30 feet high. Though large in size, the way the space was arranged conveyed a sense of coziness. The bookshelves rose in two levels to an intricate domed ceiling. Filled with books in many languages on every subject imaginable, easy access to them was provided by two rolling library ladders attached to the upper shelves. When

Pascal sat at his large, custom-made rosewood desk, he could easily see every part of the room — the entrance door, two sitting areas, the fireplace and the French doors, which led out to a spacious outdoor patio overlooking a huge swimming pool and beyond to the ocean. Adorning the marble floors were thick oriental carpets in floral designs with rich maroons, purples and greens being the dominant colors. The massive stone fireplace faced a crescent-shaped leather sofa in a deep honey color. A fully-stocked bar was built into a nearby wall.

The room conveyed a sense of understated — yet obvious — wealth, intelligence and power. As far as the books were concerned, Pascal had never read any of them. In fact, he scoffed at the notion that inherited wealth and a formal education were necessary to achieve success. Appearances, in his mind, were more important than reality. Therefore, he considered this library to be the ultimate expression of who he was. If some feared him, that was an added bonus.

When the three men entered the room, Pascal led Habib to the opulent leather sofa facing the fireplace and invited him to sit. Bernard dutifully proceeded to build a roaring fire, adding a sense of warmth to the scene, while outside, the storm raged. Bernard, as usual, stood guard at the door.

"This will make you comfortable after our time outside in the boat," said Pascal. "The storm is here and will be much worse by nightfall. Let's have drinks and I can tell you about myself and my Fortress."

"I don't mean to be forward," interjected Habib, "but I'm worried about the storm and feel we should commence our transaction now, so that I can be back at the airport this evening."

"Nonsense," responded Pascal. "We have plenty of time. I have everything under control. Trust me. Now let me tell you about this exquisite and rare Jamaican rum."

Pascal went to the bar and poured a shot glass of the expensive liquor for himself and a generous pour for Habib. Then he proceeded to explain in great detail its Jamaican origins, how much it cost, why it was so rare, and what made it distinctive from other rums. Returning to his seat by the blazing fire, Pascal, with a captive audience, was in his element, speaking knowledgeably about The Last Drop 1976 Very Old Jamaican Rum.

"This rum is considered one of the finest, most complex Jamaican rums. The Last Drop Distillery was founded in England by two elderly British friends. A single bottle can cost up to $5,500. Critics describe it as old, but vibrant and utterly delicious. Of course, a friend in the UK gifted me with an entire case." He turned to Habib and smiled. "In my business, it's all about who you know. If you play your cards right, Habib, I might even give you a bottle when we finish our business."

Habib merely nodded. He hadn't touched his rum.

"Please, Habib. Let's make a toast. This is truly a special occasion. Drink!"

Habib clinked glasses with Pascal and took a small, obligatory sip of the rum. While its taste was exquisite, he had to stay completely sober in support of his mission. "Mmm," he said. "This is lovely."

"Would you believe the founders' daughters are running the place now? I'm concerned about women running a distillery. What do they know about being in charge and maintaining a quality product? Maybe I'll buy the place from them and put my own people in charge. I've always wanted to be in the premium liquor business."

After listening patiently, Habib finally spoke up. "Thank you. You're very knowledgeable and this is excellent rum." He looked at his watch and continued. "It's late and I can see the storm is getting worse. I'd like to take a look at the cylinder seals now. Then we can conduct our business and I can be on my way."

"What's your hurry?" replied Pascal. "Isn't it your tradition to spend time getting acquainted before doing business? I certainly like to know who I'm dealing with, and I'm sure you feel the same. I'll start by telling you about myself, my beautiful Fortress and my incredible art collection," he said, taking a large sip of his drink. "Then you can fill me in on your history."

For twenty minutes, Pascal rambled on about how he'd become one of the richest men in the world. He openly bragged about how his business savvy had grown without benefit of a formal education. He talked about his various businesses, holding back only the criminal details. He boasted about how he had designed every aspect of the Fortress and how his contemporaries were openly jealous of his success. He was aware his business world included Mafia-connected enterprises, run by dangerous men — even murderers — but chose not to share this information. He didn't want to recall how fearful he often was that these men would some day put an end to his activities and his very life.

Enduring Pascal's narcissistic monologue was really getting on Habib's nerves. *Does this guy ever shut up? What's his game? Is he delaying on purpose? Or is he just showing off? Where the hell are Lance, Brad and their law enforcement back-up? I can't take much more of this.*

"Do you like women, Habib?"

"Uh, why do you ask?" countered Habib, who was

uncomfortable with the direction this conversation was taking.

"Well, I'm a man of the world and women love me. They tell me I have animal magnetism. And of course, there's my money. If you're drawn to the female sex, I can arrange pleasurable time for you with any type of woman you desire: young, old, slim, Rubenesque. I can even arrange something if men or boys are more to your taste."

Habib, horrified, kept his expression neutral. "Mr. Pascal, I'm a happily married man. Therefore, I'd prefer we conduct our business as soon as possible. Please bring the cylinder seals now so I can examine them."

Pascal waited a few beats and then moved the conversation in a completely different direction. "Did you happen to get a good look at my art collection when we walked in?"

"Of course," said Habib. "It is all museum quality. Very impressive."

"You're a man of means," said Pascal, "and you've made no secret of your admiration for the pieces you saw in the foyer. What's on display is just a small sampling of a vast collection. There's much more to see, and for the right price, all of it is available. A tour of my property will give you a more extensive perspective of its grandeur. Stay. It will take just a mere couple of hours."

Habib was spared having to answer because the library door was suddenly opened by Forrest. Having just left Nicole's quarters, he literally slinked into the room like a naughty boy who had just been chastised by an angry father.

Irritated at the interruption, Pascal glared at him with a pronounced frown, narrowing his eyes. "Is there something you need, Forrest? I told you to stay with the women."

"Yes. I should be with you to finish our deal with Mr. Habib."

"Not until you assure me the women are secure. I thought I made that clear."

"They're fine, Rene. and under Nicole's control in her quarters. The door's locked from the outside. There's no way they can escape." He paused and then added, "I see you're having drinks. May I join you?"

Pascal sniffed derisively and turned toward the bar. "You're a grown man. Help yourself!"

I thought we were business partners and friends. What could I have possibly done to deserve this demeaning treatment from Rene?

Forrest strutted to the bar, his shoulders drawn back and head held high. Only those who knew him well would know how insecure he was because of his changed status with Pascal. He grabbed a crystal tumbler and half-filled it with Pascal's expensive rum. He then moved to the curved sofa facing the fireplace and inserted himself between Pascal and Habib.

"Aren't you being a little greedy?" observed Pascal, glancing at Forrest.

The atmosphere was tense, so Habib took this opportunity to once again raise the subject of the cylinder seals.

"Mr. Pascal … about the cylinder seals?"

"All right, all right," said Pascal. Turning to Bernard, he ordered, "Please bring the case and place it on the desk."

Bernard brought the case to Pascal's large desk with Forrest right behind him. Pascal rose and summoned Habib to join him to view the treasure.

Habib's inspection was interrupted by a flash of lightning, followed by a deafening clap of thunder. Suddenly, the room went dark.

CHAPTER 36

Thunder roared and lightning streaked across the sky.

Phebe and Mallory were speechless hearing Nicole was the sister of Arthur Webster's late wife, Martine. Clearly, she was unaware that Martine had passed away. While Mallory was still feeling the effects of her fainting spell, it was Phebe who finally spoke.

"Nicole, we know this is important to you and I promise we'll share what we know soon, but now we need to focus on getting out of here."

"Yes, escaping is most important," sighed Nicole, "but Pascal said he will kill Martine if I leave him."

"Please trust us, we have friends with the FBI who can help," Phebe was quick to reply.

A disoriented Mallory was propped up in the big bed with large pillows supporting her. She had opened her eyes when she heard the woman Phebe introduced as Nicole, say something about Arthur's wife being her sister. "You said we're at Pascal's residence? He wants to kill your sister? It's so dark outside. Is it nighttime? I'm really confused trying to put the pieces together."

Sitting at her side, Phebe realized Mallory might not be able to cope with their situation. *My God! I wish I had a drink.* "A very bad storm is raging. We'd better take a minute to get you oriented, Mallory. Do you remember being at the Encanto pool?"

"Yes, I do. I also remember being rushed down a steep path to the ocean. It was very dangerous. I thought we'd fall for sure. Then, Forrest pushed us onto a boat. But after that … I just don't remember."

"You passed out on the boat and Forrest had to carry you. He was livid. I was afraid he might hurt you. Now we're locked in with Nicole. She's been a captive of Pascal's for decades." In a whisper she continued, "Her sister's name is Martine, Arthur's wife. Don't say anything. She doesn't know Martine is dead."

Suddenly, the storm announced itself again with another loud clap of thunder. Then an intense flash of lightning, so bright the room lit up as if it were midday, brought Mallory's attention to the gigantic French doors. "What's out there?" Even in her debilitated condition, Mallory knew rescue was the only way she and Phebe could survive this terrifying ordeal.

Nicole answered. "A long balcony that connects to Pascal's *salle de chambre*. When he is away, I sometimes use it to sneak into his room. That's how I found his gun. He has been using me and sharing me for sex since I was a young girl and I hate him for it. One day I will get that gun and kill him."

"Nicole, do you even know how to use his gun? If not, it could be dangerous for you." Mallory was feeling a little stronger and sat on the bedside with her feet dangling. "Phebe, I know this is a long shot, but do you still have your phone?"

Phebe pulled her cell phone from a huge side pocket in her dress. "It's right here. Things were moving so fast with the storm and the men were so busy with the buyer, they didn't bother to search me. I hope it has enough juice left to help us get out of here."

Mallory again leaned back on the pillows. "Phebe, how many people are here besides us?"

"Besides you, me and Nicole, I only know of Pascal, Forrest, Bernard, and the buyer, who came with us on the boat. Forrest has a burr up his backside because he had to carry you." Phebe looked at Nicole. "Is there anyone here with you? Are there guards?"

"Only me and two guards. They have big guns."

Mallory shivered at the thought. "Phebe, can you call Brad and tell him where we're being held?"

Phebe felt both relieved and confused when Lance answered Brad's phone. "Is this Lance? Thank God! It's Phebe. We need help. We've been kidnapped! We're trapped in a locked room on the fourth floor of Pascal's Fortress!"

"Phebe. Listen carefully. Plans are underway to rescue you. Can you help me by describing your location in more detail?" Lance's tone was curt.

"We're scared to death. Mallory passed out on the boat, but she's conscious now. The room we're in belongs to a woman named Nicole. She says she's the sister of Arthur Webster's wife. According to her, she's been a virtual prisoner for decades."

"Take a breath and focus, Phebe. Are there windows in the room?"

"There are large French doors that open to a wide balcony."

"When you look out, what do you see? Which way does the balcony face? Toward the ocean? Or, in another direction?"

"It's hard to see anything in this storm, but I can hear waves crashing, so I believe this room is facing the ocean."

"Okay. Do you have any sense of who's there besides you, Mallory, and Nicole?"

"Well there's Pascal, his man Bernard, Forrest and the man who is buying the cylinder seals. Nicole tells us there are also a couple of guards with big guns."

"You need to know the buyer, Habib, is on our side. His real name is Joe Mustafa and he's FBI."

"He must be in terrible danger. I saw Bernard had a gun." Taking a deep breath, Phebe lowered her voice and continued. "There's a room off of Nicole's that looks like a prison cell from the dark ages. I just had a quick look before Nicole made me close the door. The room is dark and windowless with heavy chains on the walls. It's terrifying. I wonder how long she's been living with this horror. She has access to Pascal's bedroom and his gun and is threatening to use it to kill him and she's desperate for us to tell her about Martine."

"You can tell her if you want, but she might lash out at you."

"Hang on a minute, Lance." Phebe addressed Nicole. "Would you please bring Mallory a glass of water?" When Nicole left the room, Phebe continued talking quietly to Lance. "We don't think she'll lash out. She's been kind to Mallory, who's been perspiring a lot; even brought her a warm washcloth and towels. I think she's had a relapse. Please hurry so we can get out of this mess alive!"

"Brad and I specifically told you not to come because of the danger. Yet, here you are, caught in the middle of this operation. Do you realize how much more difficult you've all made this rescue for us? Plus, we have the storm to deal with. We don't want anyone hurt."

"I'm sorry, Lance. Please tell Brad I'm sorry. We're all sorry."

"Sorry just doesn't cut it, Phebe."

Phebe didn't cry, but felt like it. "We didn't think this trip would be a lark. We just wanted to protect our friend. I know Mallory and I are in danger. We heard a helicopter when they forced us down the cliff from the Encanto. Was that you?"

"That helicopter is being operated by Interpol and is probably what saved your lives. We received radio intel from them that several men, including our agent, and a couple of women were forced down a cliff path to a large speedboat. That was the only information we had to go on. If Interpol can locate your room, they can lift you to their helicopter from the balcony. See if Nicole can tell you where the guards are usually stationed. We need to get you all out alive, including Pascal, who will be spending his golden years in a much smaller home."

"Nicole said the guards are always roaming around. Please be careful," pleaded Phebe.

"You have to trust that we know what we're doing. This is what I do every day and I'm good at it. Right now, I'm worried about Joe Mustafa, aka Habib. I know he didn't have a weapon when he met Pascal. I have to hang up now. The helicopter will be there soon."

The conversation with Lance did nothing to calm her nerves. *This whole situation frightens me,* worried Phebe.

Lance frightened me even further with what he said. I'm scared we won't get out of here alive. Oh my God, what next?

Phebe managed to help Mallory off the bed and onto the sofa. "Nicole, please come sit with Mallory. We want to talk to you about Martine."

Eager to hear about her sister, Nicole joined them. Phebe sat at Nicole's feet and gently took her hand.

"We never met your sister," began Mallory, "but we do know her husband, Arthur."

"Nicole," Phebe said in a soft, calm voice. "I'm so sorry to tell you this, but Arthur told us Martine is dead. We don't know the details, but we'll help you find out. That's why Pascal needed Mallory to take Martine's place as his courier."

Tears ran down Nicole's cheeks as her grip tightened on Phebe's hand. "She was the light of my life, my baby sister. All I wanted to do was to keep her safe and away from this life and these horrible people." Releasing Phebe's hand, she stood and walked toward the balcony. They heard her swear, "Pascal! I will kill you."

Phebe and Mallory sat quietly when another lightning flash caused the lights to flicker. The two sat in stark terror, enveloped in darkness.

Mallory looked around the room and saw Nicole had disappeared.

"I think Nicole must have used the balcony to go to Pascal's room," said Phebe. "Mallory, you don't think she would actually take Pascal's gun and use it? She told us she wanted to kill him."

"I'm more worried about us." Mallory patted her friend's arm. "Should we stay here?"

"That's what Lance told us to do, so the helicopter

can rescue us from the balcony."

"Did you hear that?" exclaimed Mallory. "It's different than the sounds of the storm. It sounds like the whooping of helicopter blades."

Suddenly, above the continuing sounds of the storm, gunshots rang out.

"Oh my God, no! What's happening now?" exclaimed Phebe.

"I think the guards are shooting at the helicopter."

More gunshots were heard and then silence, followed by an announcement from the helicopter. "Are you there? Come to the balcony."

"Hang on to me and we'll walk out."

The two women walked to the French doors and opened them. The helicopter, bearing an Interpol insignia, hovered near the balcony. Its side door opened, and a ladder swung out. A man began climbing down the ladder. Arriving at the balcony and seeing Mallory's condition, he called the pilot to send down a basket.

"I'm going to take her up first. I'll be right back for you." Looking at a shivering Mallory, he explained, "You'll go up in the basket. I'll be with you." Once her rescuer had Mallory inside the copter, she passed out again.

"Get the medic!"

Mallory lay on the floor at the rear of the copter. The medic put something under her nose to revive her, and she opened her eyes.

"We're taking you back to the hotel. That's what Lance said to do. Once in your room, don't go anywhere. Have the concierge call the resort's doctor. Order only from room service. Those were his explicit orders."

CHAPTER 37

Nicole was shaking as she left the women and made her way along the balcony to Pascal's suite. She would never see her beloved Martine again. *It was Pascal's fault; she was sure of it. There is no longer a reason to stay here. And no reason not to kill that bastard. It will be easy. Just pull the trigger and he will no longer exist.*

Entering his room with the key she had found years ago was easy enough. He had never missed it. Tears flowed from her eyes, causing a fog to settle over everything. No problem. She knew exactly where she was going. She stepped through the heavy drapes, letting them fall back into place behind her, muffling the sounds of the storm. This room held so much fear for her. She had endured, even pretended to enjoy his demands; his disgusting body against hers. She'd forced her mind to go elsewhere, often reliving the few good times she and Martine had enjoyed on the French Riviera, pretending to be wealthy socialites.

This would be her last time to enter this room. Thankful no one could see her, she walked past art works of female nudes to the drawer where she knew the gun and ammunition were kept. As she lifted pornographic magazines, pictures slid from between the pages and fell to the floor. Her eyes were drawn to something familiar. The pictures were of her in unspeakable situations that she didn't remember! Choking down the bile that had risen in her throat, she removed the false bottom of the drawer and pulled out the gun. It was loaded, as she knew it would be. She had been threatened with it many times.

Holding the gun within the folds of her aqua silk caftan, she entered the hall, pulling the door closed behind her. Her plan to take the elevator to the library Pascal used for visitors changed as she heard it ascending. Better still, the stairs would serve her purpose. He would not hear her coming. *I will get to him and kill him. I hope he suffers.*

Lightning flashed and thunder rumbled ever closer to the Fortress. Her clothing whipped around her as she rapidly descended the staircase. She gave no thought to the fact that Bernard or Forrest would have a weapon. She was intent only on her mission to end Pascal.

The foyer was a quick right turn as she took the last step onto the main floor. Male voices confirmed her instincts were correct. Pascal had brought the men to the library for whatever their horrid purpose was. The women had said someone was buying something from Pascal, but Nicole, through years of experience, knew that was not the only reason he had visitors.

Hidden in the shadows. she could see beyond the foyer to the library. She saw Forrest and Bernard standing around the oversized desk. Another man she didn't recognize was with them. *That must be the buyer. There is Pascal.*

Her heart pounded as she watched him open a woman's makeup case at the center of the desk. Pascal lifted a cloth from the case and as he unwrapped it, she heard the buyer draw in a deep breath.

"Have you seen anything so extraordinary in your life, Mr. Habib?" asked Pascal as he leaned against the desk.

"No, I honestly have not. I was impressed by your artwork, but these ... it's like standing in another dimension, going back in time thousands of years."

Nicole saw Pascal hand the cloth to the buyer, who lifted it closer to his eyes.

"How did you come by these seals, Mr. Pascal?"

"Oh, you needn't concern yourself with details. Are they all that you expected?"

"Yes, and more."

"Bernard, please get the laptop so Mr. Habib can finalize his purchase. As he says, he wants to get back to the airport. He is concerned with the storm and has no interest in our other entertainments. I, however, do."

Nicole raised the gun, aimed it at Pascal, and pulled the trigger again and again. The sharp popping of gunshots was muted by roaring thunder, followed by a sharp crack as lightning struck nearby, plunging the room into darkness. No matter, she was sure she'd hit her target.

Bernard snatched up the computer and grabbed his boss by the shoulder. Speaking close to his ear he said, "Those were gunshots, and they came from the foyer. Let's get out of here. Hold onto my arm," he instructed, as he turned Pascal toward the bookshelf. Bernard manually slid the bookshelf aside to reveal a secret room leading to an iron staircase. He opened it just enough for them to squeeze through. The rumble of thunder echoed through the space as they stepped onto the landing. Bernard knew the staircase went up to the rooftop as well as to the lower-level parking garage. He chose to go down. From outside the Fortress, the entrance to the garage appeared to be a simple stone wall.

Bernard hesitated to make sure they were alone. He heard no sound coming up or down from the staircase. However, he recognized the sharp slapping of helicopter blades directly overhead. The storm had knocked out the electricity and plunged the Fortress into darkness. "*Merde.* It's impossible to see anything. Hold the rail and don't let go of my arm. I will get us out of here."

Carefully they descended step by step. Entering the garage, they approached the metallic midnight blue Bugatti Chiron, always Pascal's first choice. "Not this time. Too obvious, Bernard. Let's take the truck."

Rather than getting into the truck, Pascal looked back toward the stairwell.

"There is no time to waste," Bernard said in a low voice. He held the door open for Pascal.

"Where's Forrest?" Pascal wasn't concerned with Habib because Habib had nothing to reveal to the authorities, but Forrest did.

"I was standing next to him and felt him fall. I know he didn't have a gun and neither did Habib. But I didn't search the women earlier and I doubt Forrest did."

With a shake of his head, Pascal sighed. "Nicole. It had to be Nicole. I wanted her to love me, and I treated her like a goddess, but I know she hated me. She's had plenty of time alone and may have found my Glock."

"We've got to hurry. I can hear a helicopter and sirens. They're close."

In the darkened room, and distracted by the rumble of thunder, Nicole didn't notice the open door to the hidden stairway.

Holding her breath, she carefully made her way into the library. As she approached the desk, the storm momentarily lit the room, and Nicole saw a body lying face down at her feet. Pascal! Years of hatred flashed through her mind as she gathered a mass of saliva, viciously spit on his back, then turned away. Realizing the items from the case must be valuable, she slid her hand along the desk, locating several small hard objects. Oblivious to the warm sticky liquid on the surface beneath them, she put the objects in her pocket, unconsciously wiping her hands on her gown. She didn't notice the other body lying against the back of the leather sofa.

As Nicole was leaving the library, Pascal and Bernard were preparing to make their getaway from the underground garage.

With Pascal settled on the cracked leather seat of the well-used work truck, Bernard took control of the steering wheel. Removing the gun from his waistband, he placed it in the center console within easy reach. He then stretched his arm behind the passenger seat and retrieved two sweat-stained straw hats, handing one to Pascal. His neck made an audible cracking sound as he rotated his head from shoulder to shoulder and then stretched his arm to the ignition.

"Wait," said Pascal placing his hand on Bernard's arm. "We must be extremely careful. If we leave now, they will be on us at once."

Blue lights flashed along the exterior walls of the Fortress.

Securing their bullet-proof vests, the National Police, followed by the Guardia Civil military police, descended on the Fortress in their signature Alfa Romeos. Following this caravan was a boxy yellow medical ambulance. Brad and Lance chose to travel with the Guardia Civil while Interpol agents opted for the National Police.

Having watched the property over the years, law enforcement was aware of the alternate power source. They had located the generator and gotten it running. With weapons drawn, they had checked the guard sprawled on the concrete drive and another lying close by in long grass beneath hanging bougainvillea. It took little time to declare them no longer a threat. The steel reinforced entrance door was quickly breached with the use of a hydraulic door blaster.

Pascal heard a muffled voice shouting instructions, as well as the screaming of emergency sirens. "We shall be patient," instructed Pascal. They waited until they heard the helicopter retreating into the distance. Still, Pascal kept his hand on Bernard's arm. Car doors slammed and boots pounded on marble floors as law enforcement entered Pascal's beloved sanctuary. Then silence, followed by the whirring of a generator that brought electricity back to the fortress.

"We can go now, slowly and quietly to the main road."

The military police entered first, followed by Brad and Lance. Ignoring the artwork, they moved through the foyer and into the library. Stepping past the blood-smeared desk and over a dead body, the sound of deep intermittent moaning caught their attention. Mustafa, curled into a fetal position, lay on an oriental rug, a dark liquid spreading through the floral pattern. The smoky smell of gunpowder and whiskey permeated the room.

Knees pulled to his chest and hands pressing against his left side, Mustafa gasped. "Thank God you're here! Have you found Mallory? They also kidnapped another woman. I haven't seen them since I got off the boat. Forrest said he locked them in a room upstairs."

"Try to relax, Joe," Lance said as the medics entered the room. "They'll get you out of here. The women are safe and have been airlifted to the Encanto, where they'll be medically cleared and reunited with their friends. I spoke with them on the phone," he continued. "They said another woman, Nicole, was with them, but we haven't been able to locate her."

Brad reached out to the dead body. Avoiding the blood-splattered desk, he turned the body over. "Looks like he wasn't so lucky. This is Forrest, Pascal's partner. Do you know who shot you and killed him?"

"Bernard was the only one with a gun, but he didn't have any reason to shoot any of us. We were wrapping up the deal; getting ready to transfer payment for the cylinder seals."

"Did that transfer go through?" Lance asked.

"No, the lights went out and the shots were fired." His body tightened and a muted cry escaped his lips.

"Relax. Breathe slowly."

"After the shots were fired, an angry woman entered the library and spat on that guy's back. She was sobbing and may have said, 'Pascal,' but I couldn't really understand her. Lightning flashed but I didn't see her face; only her flowing clothes. She seemed so intent on that body. I don't think she knew I was hit, or even in the room."

"What happened to Pascal and Bernard?"

"I don't know."

"I think that's the answer," said Lance, cocking his thumb toward the bookshelf that had been slid aside.

"Of course," Brad exclaimed. "Let's check it out."

Their footsteps reverberated as they made their way down the iron stairs, weapons drawn. Reaching the garage and looking around, Lance acknowledged, "This guy has more wealth than we ever imagined."

"You said it. Check out that Bugatti Chiron. The sports car next to it sure looks like it matches his boat. The jeep may be out of place, but do you smell the fumes, Lance? Looks like there was another vehicle here. They must have used it to get away."

"They haven't gotten away yet. I'll confirm with the police controlling the checkpoint." Securing the revolver in his shoulder holster, he removed the cell phone from his hip pocket and made the call. "Yes, this is Lance, FBI. Have you seen anyone leaving the area?"

"Only a couple of maintenance men in old floppy hats, driving a beat-up truck. They said they were answering a call to fix the generator at one of the estates in the area."

"That's got to be them. We fixed the generator. Let's hot wire that jeep, Brad. They can't have gotten far."

"No need. The keys are on the visor."

Back in her quarters on the fourth floor, Nicole also heard the helicopter and the sirens. *I am safe now but will never see my precious Martine again.*

Emotionally spent and out of habit, she walked out to the balcony. She knew the women had been talking to the FBI and were going to be saved. They expected her to go with them. However, the women were no longer in her room.

Standing on the balcony, she saw a helicopter disappearing into the distance and became aware of police lights in the circular drive and courtyard below. Oddly, all was now quiet. The police had entered the Fortress and the women were being flown to safety.

Looking down, Nicole saw the dented old truck as it crept out of the parking garage and wound its way around the vehicles parked outside the residence. She knew the maintenance staff used this truck but couldn't see who was inside. Anxiety rose in her chest. *I know I killed him. Who could be in this truck? No. It can't be.*

Drawn by carnal instinct, Pascal took a second to look up. There on the balcony was Nicole, staring straight at them, illuminated by the sweeping blue lights like an avenging angel. Uncharacteristically, he shuddered.

CHAPTER 38

Jesus Christ! What's taking them so long? Do you think they're okay? What were we thinking when we got ourselves into this mess?" Dana was beside herself with worry as she sprawled on the sofa in the room she shared with Phebe and Emily at the Encanto. She took one last swig directly from the bottle of wine on the end table beside her. She had drunk it all.

"Will you just chill out, Dana? There's nothing we can do and worrying doesn't help. Neither does all that wine you've drunk."

"You're right, Emily," Dana slurred her words. "I don't know why I get this way when I'm stressed."

Emily walked over to the sofa and sat down. "We have to trust Brad and Lance. They know what they're doing. All we can do is what they've asked of us — stay in our room and don't interfere."

Dana sighed. "I know. I know. I just feel so guilty thinking that we're somehow responsible for what's happened to Mallory and Phebe. And Brad. I really thought we had something special going on. I've probably screwed that up too!"

"Again, stop with the worrying and self-pity, Dana. It's not helpful."

There was a knock on the door. Emily got up and looked through the peephole, recognizing the woman who'd been at the pool earlier with Mallory. She opened the door and asked, "May I help you?"

"I'm Nina Mirelles. Maybe you'll remember I was with your friend Mallory at the pool. As I recall, you were dressed a bit differently then." She pulled out an FBI badge from her jacket pocket and showed it to Emily. "You may not know that I'm with the FBI."

"That's a surprise! Come on in. Yes, I do remember you. Why are you here?"

"I was asked to tell you your friends are safe and being brought here by helicopter," said Nina. The resort's doctor is on her way to check them out."

"Thank God! Did you hear that, Dana?"

"What a relief!" Dana took a deep breath and willed herself to relax.

The medics arrived with Mallory on a stretcher, and Phebe and Dr. Alvaro, Encanto's in-house physician, following close behind. Carefully placing Mallory on one of the beds, the medics set up an IV and placed a needle into her arm. Dr. Alvaro took over as she began to stir.

Dana, wracked with sobs, wrapped her arms around Phebe, while Emily gathered them both in a tight embrace.

"You have no idea how worried we were," exclaimed Dana. "How did we ever get ourselves into this mess?"

"No worries, Dana. We're all adults and we made the

best decision we could as a group, based on the circumstances. It wasn't about us; we were laser-focused on supporting Mallory. We're all safe now, but Mallory has been through a terrible ordeal."

The women sat, as Phebe recounted the events of the afternoon. She began with her abduction by Forrest.

"Pascal and his men took Mallory down the cliff path. My disguise didn't fool Forrest. He recognized me right away, grabbed me by the arm and forced me to go along."

"We wondered where you'd gone," said Emily. "We were watching the rescue of a little boy who almost drowned. When I turned around to look for you, Pascal and his group were gone. And so were you."

Dana's phone rang. It was Detective Dave Elliott calling from Palm Springs.

"Dana? I've been trying to contact Brad and he isn't picking up. Do you know where he is?"

"Not exactly. He and Lance and a whole bunch of cops have gone to Pascal's residence to arrest him. I imagine they're there now. You have no idea what a day this has been!"

"I have information he'll want to hear. Is anyone else there from the FBI I can speak with?"

"Here's Agent Nina Mirelles," she said, handing Nina her cell phone.

Nina stepped out of the room to take the call. Detective Elliott informed her that Martine Webster's body had been exhumed and autopsied. The cause of death was now determined to be homicide. She'd been given a lethal dose of insulin, which had disappeared from her blood after she died, rendering it undetectable. Hence, the initial determination of suicide. With the recent autopsy, the coroner found a previously undetected injection site. He tested the tissues surrounding it and found markedly high levels of the hormone. Martine was not a diabetic and had no reason to be using insulin.

"Please pass this along to Lance and Brad as soon as possible and ask them to give me a call. Don't share this information with anyone else before they're made aware."

"Copy that," replied Nina.

As Nina returned to the hotel room, Dana immediately demanded, "What did he say? Has something happened we should know about?"

"All in good time," Nina responded, standing near the door. "That information is for Lance and Brad's ears only. Nothing for you to be concerned with." And as suddenly as she'd arrived, she abruptly turned to leave, saying, "I have a plane to catch. I'm outta here."

Standing in the rain on the balcony at the Fortress, Nicole was in a frenzy of mixed emotions: relief at finally killing her tormentor; grief at losing her sister; confusion at all the chaos surrounding her; and finally fear, at what would come next. She had no intention of going to prison, but knew she'd be arrested as soon as the police found her and discovered she'd fired the shot that killed Pascal. Luckily, she'd had the presence of mind to stash the tiny art objects she'd grabbed from Pascal's library. They were safely hidden in an ancient urn on a table in the hallway just outside Pascal's room. She would retrieve them later if the police believed her story about the years she'd been held in captivity.

What next? she asked herself. *They'll be here soon. I can't really escape this place. I have nowhere to go.* Her desperation sparked an idea.

As the rain became more intense, she re-entered her bedroom soaking wet, toweled off, put on a bathrobe and made herself comfortable on the couch. *When they get here I will simply tell the truth. I've been Pascal's prisoner since I was a young girl. He used me till I began to age and then went after Martine. I'm convinced he's responsible for her death. He ruined our lives and I'll never forgive him. He was a monster! If the authorities have an ounce of compassion, there's a small glimmer of hope I'll survive this nightmare!*

She reached into her pocket, pulled out Pascal's Glock, removed the bullets and laid the gun and ammunition carefully on the coffee table in front of her. Then, she waited.

Bernard drove carefully through the stormy darkness. The truck helped disguise them for the moment, but eventually the police would realize who they were and come racing after them with everything they had. They had to move fast and get to safety. But where?

As he meandered through the streets of Puerto de Pollensa adjoining the marina, Bernard thought they were safe. They'd made it through the checkpoint without being detained. The old maintenance truck and their sweat-stained straw hats had done the trick. The rain was still pouring down and the picturesque resort town had already rolled up its sidewalks for the night, so no partiers were evident on the streets. Bernard found himself approaching the Ma-2200 highway. He would have to turn left to go south in order to leave the area and head toward safety in Palma.

Looking through his rear-view mirror, Bernard noticed a Jeep speeding toward them.

"You have to get on the main highway!" shrieked Pascal. "Otherwise we'll be forced to take the Formentor

Road. It dead ends at the lighthouse!"

"Relax, Rene. I know what I'm doing," Bernard responded in a calm voice. "I've got this."

"Maybe not," shouted Pascal, as he saw what awaited them down the highway. Police cars, with their lights blazing, had set up another check point, effectively leaving them no option but to take the dangerous road to Cape Formentor.

"That's them just ahead," Lance pointed from the passenger's seat. "With all those flashy cars in the garage, who would've thought they'd escape in an old pickup truck!"

"That was a good choice and bought them time." Brad tightened his grip on the steering wheel. "With that checkpoint blocking the road, they have two options — be captured or take the road toward the Formentor Lighthouse. From what I've heard, it's seven miles of a narrow, winding road with high cliffs dropping to the ocean — definitely not recommended for someone with vertigo. We have a wild ride ahead of us."

"Then I'm glad you're at the wheel and not me," answered Lance. "This blasted storm doesn't help a bit. The road will be slippery with lots of switchbacks. I don't know how well it's lighted."

"We have the advantage, though. We're driving a new all-terrain Jeep and they're in an old jalopy!"

"Don't be so sure. Those two are probably familiar with every twist and turn."

Brad sped up and, as he'd predicted, saw the truck turn toward the lighthouse. "Hold on tight and make sure your seat belt is secure. Maybe we can catch them before they reach the switchbacks."

Though ill-prepared for a speed chase in a truck, Bernard was, as Brad suspected, thoroughly acquainted with this road. Ever the faithful bodyguard, he'd scouted it as an escape route many times, just in case he would ever need it.

Over the past few minutes, the storm had grown stronger, bringing more lightning and fierce winds. Even with windshield wipers on full speed, it was almost impossible to see the road.

Brad turned on his high beams, creating a glare in the truck's rearview mirror, which made it more difficult for Bernard to see where he was going. The two vehicles made their way onto the cape, with the Jeep several car lengths behind. Bernard, with his knowledge of the road, suddenly shot ahead and disappeared around a curve.

Rounding the curve, Brad noticed the road extended steeply upward in a series of switchbacks. He caught sight of the truck in the distance and was frustrated it was making good time on the straightaways and slowing down for the hairpin curves.

"Whoever's driving that truck knows what he's doing. I suspect the driver is Pascal's man, Bernard." Another bolt of lightning lit the sky, followed by a rumble of thunder, creating a momentary distraction. Brad could see the truck was rapidly gaining speed and would soon reach the top and disappear into the distance. He sped up as much as he dared, but he was no match for Bernard's superior driving skills.

"Slow down, for God's sake. Are you trying to kill us?" screamed Pascal, as Bernard increased his speed, barely maintaining control of the rickety old truck as it swayed with each curve.

"I know what I'm doing. I have a plan."

"A plan won't help if we're careening off a cliff and falling into the sea. I'm not ready to die!" Pascal was terrified and reaching his breaking point.

It took Brad a couple of minutes to make his way to the top of the incline, where the road momentarily straightened out. The truck was nowhere in sight. He drove a little faster now. Rounding a gentle curve, he finally caught sight of it speeding off into the distance.

Even in the darkness, the men could see the truck swerving out of control and arcing off the road and over the cliff, toward the raging sea below.

CHAPTER 39

It's as if the fucking storm never took place!" Lance was pacing back and forth frustrated, as he surveyed the scene in front of them. "What in the hell happened here?"

Last night's storm had made it impossible for local police to do any more than close the highway and secure the area. The present day had dawned clear and sunny. Aside from a few stray puddles, the road was dry. The only sign that something strange had occurred the night before were tire tracks through the low shrubs and loose rocks where the truck had left the highway before plunging off the cliff. There were no skid marks on the pavement to indicate Bernard had used his brakes.

The site was literally crawling with law enforcement. The Formentor Road, so forbidding and dangerous in last night's storm, appeared almost peaceful in the light of day. To preserve evidence, the road would be closed to the public until the investigation was complete.

Brad shared Lance's frustration. "I thought we had them when they were forced to drive toward the lighthouse," he said. "Unfortunately, we underestimated Bernard's knowledge of the road. Do you think they intentionally went off the cliff?"

"We'll know more when we retrieve the wreckage and find their bodies," answered Lance.

"If we find their bodies," groused Brad.

Pascal's truck had nose-dived from the sheer granite cliff into deep, roiling water. There were no beaches or coves on this side. Bits and pieces of the small vehicle were being tossed about in the eddies below, but no signs of human life were visible.

Back at the Fortress, a different scene was playing out.

Searching the Fortress had taken most of the night, and it was dawn before a police officer finally reached Nicole's locked quarters on the fourth floor. Using a pry bar, it took him merely seconds to enter the elegant room and find himself face to face with Nicole. Perfectly composed, considering the circumstances, the delicate woman showed no fear. On the coffee table in front of the sofa were a Glock pistol and its ammunition, which the agent immediately retrieved.

He spoke into his radio. "Guys, you'd better get in here." He gave directions and soon the other members of his team joined him in the spacious suite.

"Ma'am? Are you okay?"

"*Oui*," she responded.

"Are you Nicole?"

She nodded her head.

"Come with me," beckoned the agent. "You're safe now. We'll have a medic check you out and then we'll want to ask you some questions."

And just like that, Nicole was led out of the room willingly and peacefully. As she was taken away from the Fortress and driven to FBI headquarters in Palma, she breathed a sigh of relief. For the first time in decades, she felt truly free.

Later, Brad and Lance met with Mallory, Phebe, Emily and Dana in their room at the Encanto and brought them up to speed.

Mallory bombarded them with questions. "Please tell us what happened last night. Were you able to arrest Pascal, Forrest and their men? What's the story with Nicole? Is she really the sister of Arthur's wife? What happened to your man, Mustafa?"

Lance took a few minutes to describe the dramatic events of the previous night.

"Are you kidding me?" said Mallory. "Are you sure they drove off a cliff? Why would they do that? Did you find any bodies? After all we've been through, I'd hoped for a more satisfying result!"

"No bodies yet," said Brad, "but it's just a matter of time before they'll be found. No one could survive something like that."

"Don't be too sure," countered Emily. "I've known men like that. They're like cockroaches. No matter what happens to them, they keep crawling back!"

Mallory asked, "What about your agent, Mustafa? Did he carry out the sale of the cylinder seals?"

"No," answered Lance. "The transaction was interrupted by a woman who shot him and killed Forrest Williams."

"A woman? Could it have been Nicole? She was the only woman there besides Mallory and me and she had access to Pascal's gun. She swore she would use it to kill him. She said he'd kept her captive for years and abused her with drugs, sex and torture. She blamed him for Martine's death." Pausing for a moment, she then asked, "Is Mustafa going to be all right?"

"He's been taken to the hospital. The doctor told us his injury was serious, but not life-threatening. We'll be checking in on him later today."

"Thank goodness!"

Mallory had one more question for Lance. "Where is Nina Mirelles and what's her story? Pascal told me she was his 'associate' and suggested her presence with me on the plane was no accident. You said she worked for the FBI. She was just here a few minutes ago. Does that mean she's a double agent?"

"She's worked for us for a long time and has been an undercover operative with Pascal's operation for the past several months. Apparently, she's gained his trust, but has been unable to provide information to us so far because he's been watching her so closely. Despite the challenges, I find her completely reliable."

"If she's so reliable, where is she now?"

"Don't worry about Nina. She's probably already on her way back to DC."

"I don't know," mused Mallory. "For some reason, I don't trust her."

Lance excused himself to follow up with the coroner, who would perform an autopsy on Forrest to determine the cause of death. It was obvious he was shot, but removing the bullet would establish whether the bullet came from the gun found earlier in Nicole's room.

Brad lingered behind and asked Dana if she would step

out to the balcony with him for a private conversation. Once there, the two embraced and Dana burst into tears.

"Brad, I've made an absolute mess of things," she sobbed. "I'm so sorry we've complicated your investigation."

"I'm just happy none of you are hurt."

"Mallory's going to be traumatized by this for a long time. Toni took advantage of her desperate financial situation. Mallory never intended to get mixed up with Forrest and Pascal. She tried every way she could to stay out of it. She's a good person who got caught up in something beyond her control."

"I know," he said, holding her tighter. "Look. Before this whole thing started, you and I were just getting to know each other and I felt real chemistry between us. Is that still true for you?"

"Yes. But there are some dark things about me that you don't know. I'm scared to move forward with you until I've figured it out."

"Take all the time you need," he said. "I can be very patient." He looked into her eyes and moved in for a lingering kiss. "Let's talk more when we get back to Palm Springs."

Back at the scene of the accident on the Formentor Road, law enforcement was finishing up its investigation. In the water below, a Guardia Civil speedboat was attempting to retrieve evidence from the crash, but the rough sea wasn't cooperating. A flotilla of small boats had also gathered. Most of the looky lous were curious tourists and nosy locals. One small boat pulled away from the rest and headed out to sea. The sole occupant was Nina Mirelles. On the padded bench seat behind her was a large art portfolio, practically bursting at the seams. A furtive smile lit up her face as she pondered her future.

229

CHAPTER 40

It was an unusually balmy day as Brad walked into the Palm Springs Police Station and headed straight for Dave Elliott's office. Standing at Dave's door, he looked in and watched him end a rather heated phone conversation.

"Am I interrupting?"

Dave smiled, motioned for Brad to come in and stood to greet him.

"Brad! It's good to have you back!"

"You have no idea how good it feels to be back in the good old USA."

"Take a load off and have a cup of very bad coffee."

"Thanks Dave." Brad sat down and the two took time to exchange a few pleasantries.

Brad finally got down to business. "I'm here to tie up as many loose ends as possible. First, the date ranch. I understand the joint effort between the Palm Springs Police and the DEA recently uncovered a huge shipment delivered to the property. Evidently that ranch was the holding place for drugs Pascal's network stole from one of the cartels."

"You're right. They found massive quantities of cocaine, heroin, and enough fentanyl to decimate the entire population of Palm Springs. The Mexican cartel who brokered those shipments is out for revenge. One of our confidential informants told me whoever's responsible is dead meat when they're found."

"Well, Forrest is dead, and Pascal … we just don't know. Lance and I think he and his man Bernard drowned in the channel off the Formentor peninsula in Mallorca. Their truck hurtled over a steep cliff into very rough waters. Interpol and the Mallorcan police searched for days and recovered debris from his vehicle, but no human remains."

"No loss to the public," Dave commented.

"I feel the same way, but I'd like to know for sure. The death of any drug czar would potentially save many innocent lives."

"True." Dave walked over to the coffee machine and gave Brad a cup while taking one for himself.

"Thanks. You know this all started because of a séance in Idyllwild. That's where I met Dana, Mallory and Phoebe. Even your friend, Arthur Webster, was there. I was working undercover on a drug-related case that had nothing to do with Forrest or Pascal's operation. I'd been in New Orleans tracking a low-level drug dealer named Alex Dunbar and followed him to the Coachella Valley. Turns out he was the medium conducting the séance. To top it off, he had somehow morphed into a beautiful female calling herself Annalore Dubois! We found out later Dunbar had made plans for sex change surgery, funded by his drug money. It was well past the time the séance was scheduled to start, so everyone thought Ms. Dubois would be a no show. Finally, she rushed in with a threat: 'There will be no séance tonight, but be warned. One of you will die and another will be charged with murder.' We barely had time to understand what she'd said before she vanished into the night. I thought she must have been aware an agent was on her trail, so she chose that dramatic opportunity to get out of there. Still, her words were prophetic because someone died and someone else — Mallory — may well be charged with murder."

Dave thought for a moment, then spoke. "Brad, a fatal accident was reported recently in the local mountains. A body and a partially burned car were found in a ravine just off Highway 74. The driver must have died upon impact. Besides what remained of the body, the only thing that survived intact was a crystal ball. The coroner did an autopsy and a DNA test. The body was dressed as a woman, but the autopsy revealed otherwise. Perhaps that is your Alex Dunbar."

"If it is, that would close my original assignment in Palm Springs. When do they expect the DNA results?" Brad asked, as he looked at his coffee cup, sniffed the contents with a frown and set it down on Dave's desk.

"It'll probably take another week or two."

"That's good to hear. There's another twist," Brad continued. "While we were in Mallorca, we found Martine Webster's sister, Nicole. Just as Arthur told you, she'd been held captive by Pascal since she was a young woman. A torture chamber adjoined her bedroom, and I can only imagine the horrors she must have suffered there. She told us Pascal said as long as Martine continued to courier for him, he'd keep her safe. If she didn't, well … Nicole didn't know what would happen."

"Yes, Pascal tormented the sisters for years," Dave added. "Arthur showed me Martine's diary, which explains a lot about them. He agreed to have Martine's body exhumed for a second autopsy and samples from the first autopsy were evaluated with the most recent technology. I relayed the findings to the FBI in Mallorca. The coroner found she'd been dosed with insulin, causing her death. He reclassified her death from a heart attack to murder."

"Yes, Dave. I did get that information. Unfortunately, it may be difficult to determine who injected her."

After taking a sip of his coffee, Dave agreed, "We may never be able to prove it, but since she refused to keep couriering for Pascal, no doubt he was responsible. Now tell me, how's Mallory doing? I understand she's going to have to make a court appearance next week."

"Thank God it's not this week! Dana tells me she's not doing too well. She's been kept in bed since she arrived home in Palm Springs. Her friends have set up a wall of protection around her. Toni Vitale made serious accusations against her, Dave. I'm glad we have the pictures of Mallory's neck where Toni tried to choke her."

"Brad, when you meet with Mallory, I'd like to have Arthur join you. He has a friend named Jessica Cruz-Rodrigues, an exceptional defense attorney, who lives and practices here in the area and in Los Angeles. She handles high profile cases and has been very successful. Arthur spoke to her, and she's extremely interested in hearing more. She may even be willing to take Mallory's case pro bono."

"That sounds like an excellent idea! We'll be meeting at Mallory's home tomorrow at 10 a.m. Let's hope she's up for it. She's very fragile and endured difficult challenges in Mallorca. And it was all my fault. I recruited her, even though she was still recovering from her kidnapping! While under Forrest and Pascal's control, she was pushed down a treacherous cliff path to Pascal's speedboat. Then, she was forced to sit at the back of the boat, where she was drenched in freezing salt water. Did you know she became so weak she had to be airlifted in a helicopter back to the Encanto to be with her friends and medically checked out? Our agent in Mallorca, Joe Mustafa, said Pascal treated Forrest like a servant. My guess is that Forrest was so angry with Pascal and his condescending attitude, he took it out on Mallory. Phebe told us Forrest carried Mallory over his shoulder like a sack of potatoes."

"He didn't physically hurt her, did he?"

"No, he just threatened her."

"How is Mustafa doing? You said he was injured."

"Yes, he was shot up badly and is now recuperating in a hospital in Palma. Joe was an excellent choice to replace the real buyer and played his part well. Lance and I know he'll be there a few weeks before getting back to work. He says he can't wait to get back inside Pascal's Fortress and inventory the stolen art and artifacts. It will take months, if not longer, for him to get the art sorted and classified, and who knows when everything will be returned to the rightful owners."

Brad stood. "Well, we've gotten a few things cleared up. I look forward to the meeting at Mallory's tomorrow. Dana thinks she's still too weak to manage a courtroom or a judge, so I hope this meeting won't overwhelm her."

"Brad, I feel she'll be comfortable being around friends who are doing their best to support her. That circle of friends also includes you, Lance, and Arthur. You all have her best interests at heart and will be able to provide helpful information about the case and the possibility of getting her a good attorney."

"Well, I'd better be on my way. I'm betting the coffee at Mallory's tomorrow will be better than that swill you've forced on me today."

Brad laughed and then got serious. "Tomorrow's meeting will be a big step in getting Mallory cleared of all charges against her. She's actually a hero. We hadn't had much luck nailing Pascal and weren't even aware of Forrest until Mallory came into the picture. Rather than being charged with any crime, she should be rewarded."

"Agreed!" Dave smiled. "Looks like you'll be able to return to Washington soon."

"We'll see about that. Things don't always turn out the way we expect. I have one more stop to make before calling it a day."

CHAPTER 41

Brad drove the short distance along South Palm Canyon Drive to Dana's condo. There was something serious she wanted to discuss privately and she said Koffi, where they'd met previously, was too public.

A strong man, he nevertheless had an uneasy feeling, uncertain what the personal matter might be. He liked Dana — really liked her — and he hoped this new relationship wasn't coming to a premature end.

Mountains towering above the desert floor provided a dramatic backdrop, and a gentle breeze ruffled his salt and pepper hair as he approached the dusty orange terracotta door marked with a bronze number 6. Dana had explained she'd moved here after her husband's death. She said they'd had a wonderful marriage, so he understood she was probably still grieving.

Encouraged to see she was security conscious, he pressed the button on the Ring doorbell. Knowing she might see him through the camera app, he smiled.

"Hi Brad. I'm happy you agreed to meet here instead of Koffi. I don't want others to overhear a conversation that's very difficult for me."

Brad leaned forward, expecting to exchange a hug. Dana, however, had already turned, saying over her shoulder, "Let's go out by the pool. It's quiet there, and the breeze is pleasant."

Sitting on the pool deck gave them the privacy she desired.

"Brad, I've been wanting to talk to you about my drinking problem, but it never seemed to be the right time. You may have noticed I get a bit tipsy when under pressure."

He was relieved but concerned at the same time. This was an intimate disclosure, and he didn't want to screw things up by saying something wrong.

"I wondered if you ever might want to talk about that."

"I may have killed someone," she blurted. Catching her breath, tears began streaming down her cheeks.

"What are you talking about? You aren't capable of such a thing."

"I spent time with friends in Lake Arrowhead for Thanksgiving and drank too much. I remember driving over a big bump, but don't recall anything else about the drive home. Later, terrifying nightmares began and continue to this day." She hesitated.

"I know it must be hard for you, but please go on. Tell me about the nightmares."

"I'm driving down a dark mountain road, like the one I took that night. It's foggy — really foggy. I can barely make out the middle line in the road. I know I should have spent the night in Lake Arrowhead, but I didn't. The alcohol affected my better judgment."

"Alcohol has a way of doing that," Brad said.

Dana continued. "In the nightmare, I feel a bump against the grill. The car swerves to the right and jolts me into the dashboard. I've hit something hard. Finding my way to the side of the road, I park and get out of the car. It's impossible to see or even hear anything in the dark heavy fog.

"I'm scared. The situation is unfamiliar and I'm alone. So, I get back in the car and slowly make my way home. Each time I have this nightmare, the fear that I hit a person becomes more real. I honestly think I may have killed someone. The papers haven't reported any stories about an accident in the mountains but that doesn't mean there wasn't one, and my car does have a large dent in the bumper I can't explain. I hate driving now."

Brad's law enforcement instincts kicked in as he asked, "When did this happen? Have you contacted the local police?"

"No Brad. I've been frozen with fear about this. I know it sounds cowardly and uncaring."

"Do you recall the date this happened?"

Dana ran her fingers through her spiky hair. "It was last November. November 23rd. I'll never forget it."

Taking the phone from his breast pocket, Brad held up his index finger and said, "Hang on a minute, I have a friend assigned to the Running Springs station of the Highway Patrol. We may get lucky. If he's on duty he could shed light on this."

Dana sat quietly as Brad explained the situation to his friend, providing the date and time. He asked if there were any unusual occurrences that night on the local roads near Lake Arrowhead.

After listening for a few moments, Brad turned to Dana.

"Jerry's put me on hold while he does a quick computer search. If anything was reported on that date, it won't take long for him to find it."

Brad saw Dana's knuckles turn white as she nervously clutched her hands in her lap.

"Dana, please try to relax. No problem is so large it can't be sorted out by facing it directly.

"Here we go, he's back on the line," Brad continued. He listened and then said, "Jerry, I'm going to put you on speaker. There's someone here who would be relieved to hear this information. Can you repeat it, please?"

"Yes, of course," answered Jerry. "As I was saying, that was one of the foggiest nights we'd experienced for a long time. In fact, a small deer had been hit and was found when the fog cleared in the morning. In the past, we'd immediately remove it from the road, have the meat processed and donate it to local food banks. Now we must contact the Department of Transportation because of health and habitat concerns. They have an eco-friendly method of disposing of it. That's how it works these days and that's what we did in this case.

"The vehicle is another matter," he continued. "I imagine the car suffered damage that had to be dealt with, but we have no report of it. Does this information clear up your friend's concerns?"

"Yes. Thanks, buddy. Much appreciated. I'll be in touch."

Dana's shoulders slumped and with a sigh, she released a breath she was unaware of holding.

"I know you must be relieved Dana, and I'm happy no person was involved."

"Brad, you have no idea how reassuring this is." Dana looked away taking a deep breath. "I know I still need help with my drinking." She once again ran her fingers through her hair, raising it a bit higher, accentuating the bold blond streaks. "I've always been confident and outgoing, but I started drinking to forget the pain of losing my husband. Then after the accident, with the nightmares, it just got out of control."

"I understand you want to get out of the habit of drinking your fears away and I don't want to overstep. You must be aware there is a great rehab center in Rancho Mirage."

"I do know, and it has an exceptional reputation. It's worth giving them a call before we talk more about it. Thank you, Brad, I really appreciate your support and thanks for not judging me. That means a lot. "

As they stood, Brad lightly touched her back as he had done at the coffee shop. He felt a bolt of electricity still and hoped she did as well.

"I can offer you lemonade. That's all I have in the house now."

"I'd love a lemonade," he smiled.

As they entered the cozy kitchen, he folded his 6'2" frame into what now looked like a tiny dinette chair at the round glass table.

Dana asked, "Now that your assignment here in Palm Springs is wrapping up, when will you be returning to Washington?"

"Dana, that's something I've been thinking about very seriously. I even discussed it with my brother, Chuck, who seems to worry I'll end up a sad old bachelor with a cat living in my studio apartment in DC."

Brad's words brought a huge smile to Dana's face. "Good Lord! That isn't what I envisioned for you at all."

"So, you've been thinking about me? That's good to hear, Dana. I know I told you my work as a dedicated civil servant was mostly boring. That isn't quite true. I was often an undercover operative, which means I led a dual existence for extended periods of time. I felt it would be unfair to bring a woman into my chaotic and dangerous life. Yes, I've had relationships, but nothing long term."

Moving the peace plant from the center of the glass table and raising her bright blue eyes directly to his steel gray ones, she replied, "I've had a recent taste of that life as a nun, and definitely understand the stress you must be under much of the time."

"Dana, that's true. But lately I've been thinking it's possible to change my life. After twenty-five years with the department, I could retire comfortably and pursue my first love, the law. I passed the bars in Washington and California and managed to keep the licenses active over the years. Being a consultant for a local firm is doable and would allow me to set my own hours."

"Oh Brad! How exciting for you."

"After seeing Chuck's settled life, I realize what I've been missing. I'd love to find a permanent home — hopefully, right here in the desert. Dana, to be honest, meeting you has changed how I feel and think about a lot of things. Maybe I'm moving a little too fast. I don't want to frighten you and don't expect any commitment from you now. Let's see where we go from here. It could be an enjoyable ride."

"Brad, you aren't scaring me at all and I'm ready to take that ride with you; wherever it may lead."

CHAPTER 42

If one didn't know otherwise, one might assume the group gathered at Mallory's home was just a friendly reunion of the same folks who'd first met at the failed séance in Idyllwild.

Just as it was then, the group included a diverse mix of characters.

There were the three longtime friends — Mallory, Dana and Emily — who had attended the séance out of curiosity and a need to escape the desert heat. Phebe Wahl, a new arrival from points east, had left a doomed relationship to seek a fresh start and new friends in Southern California. DEA agent Brad Merrill, from Washington DC, had been working undercover on a drug case that involved the medium, Annalore Dubois. Lance Harris, an FBI agent investigating art theft, was also working undercover, posing as a student. Finally, there was Arthur Webster, a distinguished retiree and widower, who had attended in a desperate attempt to connect spiritually with his late wife, Martine.

Only two people were missing from the original group: Roger and Grace Chen, a grieving couple who had just lost a son. Art dealers from San Francisco, they had been the target of Lance Harris' investigation at the time. Lance had discovered the Chens were innocent of any wrongdoing.

When Lance and Brad determined the FBI and DEA were investigating the same criminal, they had partnered up and formed a joint task force. Said criminal — Rene Pascal — was involved in numerous criminal activities: drug smuggling, human trafficking and stolen art, to name a few. The investigation led them to Mallorca, where the women gathered today found themselves thrust into grave danger.

The mood among the group assembled in Mallory's living room was a complicated mix of joy and dread; joy that they had survived and succeeded in securing many stolen art treasures; and dread because Mallory was now entangled in a legal quagmire that could land her in prison. It had been a long, grueling journey that had brought them from the séance to this place and there were still loose ends to clear up. Today they would review the aftermath of their journey and create a plan that could ensure Mallory's freedom.

Arthur had brought a friend to the gathering — Jessica Cruz-Rodrigues, a criminal defense attorney.

Comfortably seated in Mallory's spacious living room, they looked out on her beautiful garden and swimming pool. Lance stood, drawing everyone's attention as he began speaking.

With a nod to Mallory, he said, "Thank you all for agreeing to meet here. Given Mallory's condition, it made the most sense."

He paused and made eye contact with each person in the room. "First, an update on the case. Joe Mustafa, who stepped up to assume the buyer's identity with Pascal, was badly wounded and is recovering in a hospital in Palma. He's eager to track down the rightful owners of the stolen art works. Once they're located, the process of repatriation will begin. The cylinder seals will be returned to the Iraqi Museum.

"We know Pascal held Nicole, Marni's sister, in captivity for years. A beautiful woman, she was surrounded by all the trappings of wealth — beautiful clothes, a luxurious home, the finest food. To an outsider, she seemed to have everything … everything, that is, except her freedom and dignity. She was Pascal's property, to do with as he wished. He controlled her using medieval devices in an archaic torture room."

A momentary expression of disgust appeared on Cruz-Rodrigues' face. A single tear ran down Arthur's cheek.

"During a massive storm, Nicole shot and killed Forrest, believing he was Pascal and, in the darkness, unknowingly shot Joe. She also protected Mallory and Phebe — complete strangers — during their capture. Now it's our turn to protect her."

Arthur spoke. "I had no idea! What can I do to help?"

"Arthur," said Lance, "the Agency has resources available for victims of violent crime. Nicole certainly qualifies, especially since she's provided us with valuable information about Pascal's enterprises. For now, she's being sequestered in one of our safe houses in Palma. She told us she's looking forward to meeting you. Perhaps a few weeks' visit to Palm Springs would give her a chance to get acquainted with you and learn about the life you and Marni shared."

"Of course! I consider her family. She'll be quite comfortable and safe here. Phebe and Mallory can help her adapt to desert living."

"Dana and I can help too," Emily chimed in.

"Arthur," continued Lance, "that's a kind offer and could go a long way toward making Nicole feel safe. The Bureau will arrange her travel."

Arthur nodded his thanks.

Lance continued with his case update. "So far, we've found no signs of Pascal and his man, Bernard, though we've searched the wreckage site thoroughly. We're convinced they couldn't have survived the plunge from the cliff. We'll continue our investigation to ensure they're no longer a threat."

Mallory tried to stay awake but kept nodding off. Engaging with people and reliving the horrors of the Mallorca trip had exhausted her.

Lance could see he was losing her and spoke up. "Mallory. Let's address your situation."

Mallory's eyes fluttered open as she looked his way. "Yes, please. I'm being arraigned next week and I'm scared to death!"

"Jessica?" Lance said, looking at Arthur's guest. "I'm going to turn this over to you."

Earlier, Arthur had introduced the attorney to Mallory and her friends, offering a summary of her many qualifications and successes in the courtroom.

"Mallory," Jessica began, "I'm happy to be here. After Arthur briefed me on your case I was able to obtain copies of the files. I'm confident I can help you."

A big smile lit up Mallory's pale face. Though exhausted and still weak from her recent ordeal, she had taken time to put on a colorful caftan, sandals, and a beaded bracelet.

She had showered, washed and brushed her hair to a shiny sheen and even applied a little lipstick. "I'm so glad you're here, Jessica, and I'm grateful for anything you can do for me."

Jessica continued, "I've spent a great deal of time reviewing your case and I'm willing to work pro bono. The charges against you are based on the circumstances surrounding Toni's death and the contents of the folder found at her home. The prosecution team is following the facts and investigating thoroughly. We have little doubt the information against you is false — completely fabricated by Toni. If so, the truth will eventually be revealed. She appeared to be collecting information on you and others and twisting it for her own purposes — probably with blackmail in mind. It seems Toni was jealous of your success in the art world and especially, your long, happy marriage to her ex-husband. When she called you to her home that night, it was obvious the two of you had a physical encounter.

"A photo taken of you at the hospital shows scratches and bruises on your neck, supporting your account of what happened that night. Your struggle with Toni and the long scarf found at her home is likely what caused those injuries. DNA evidence from the scarf may lend credence to this theory."

"What will happen to me?"

"If things turn out as I suspect, the charges against you will be dropped and you'll be free to resume your life. You scored a lot of points with the authorities when you agreed to go to Mallorca. In fact, it's likely the government will grant you a reward for your cooperation in the Pascal case."

Mallory sighed and slumped in her chair. "What a huge relief! I've been terrified about the prospect of spending the rest of my life in prison. It'll be good to have you by my side at next week's arraignment."

"Of course! I'll ask for a continuance to give us plenty of time to prepare."

Mallory smiled and wiped away a tear. The group began to stir with a new energy, beginning to see light at the end of a long, dark tunnel.

"Come on, people!" exclaimed Brad. "This is a celebration, not a wake. We have much to be thankful for." Pointing to a large wooden table in the adjoining room, he added, "I suggest we eat and socialize!"

"Yes!" said Phebe. "We've arranged a buffet breakfast. There's coffee, tea and fresh juice from Mallory's orange trees. Emily has whipped up a lovely Quiche Lorraine and there's also a big platter of fresh fruit. Help yourselves to scones and bagels and don't forget to have some sausage and bacon."

Emily popped open a bottle of champagne and poured celebratory mimosas. Dana made a point of declining the bubbly and stuck with her juice. She glanced at Brad, who knowingly nodded his head and smiled.

The group was now abuzz with lively conversation and there was an atmosphere of gaiety. Mallory clinked her glass with a spoon to get everyone's attention.

"I'm so thankful you all supported me through this nightmare. Emily and Dana, you know I think of you as sisters."

"We wouldn't have had it any other way," Emily said. At that moment she heard a ding on her phone signaling a text had arrived. She excused herself and stepped out the door to the garden terrace.

"Phebe," Mallory went on, "not only did you become a trusted member of our sisterhood, when you became my tenant, you helped me in practical ways."

Looking at Phebe and Dana, she continued. "You two and Emily risked your lives by following me to Mallorca, which I consider a real act of love."

She was tiring, but wanted to continue.

"Brad, despite what happened with Toni, you gave me a chance to redeem myself by sending me to Mallorca. You convinced me I was strong enough to help you bring Pascal down."

"It was my pleasure," responded Brad. "My trust in you never wavered."

"Lance. For someone who looks like a teen-ager, you are a strong leader. You guided me through every step.

"And Arthur. Though you were grieving for Martine, you requested a second look at her death, never believing such a bright spirit was capable of suicide. You also connected my friends with Dave Elliott, who was so helpful during my kidnapping. At last you have something positive to look forward to in getting to know your sister-in-law, Nicole."

"Absolutely! When she visits, I'll take you all out to dinner so we can get to know each other under more favorable conditions."

As the party gained momentum, there was lightness in the air, signaling an end to the ugly chaos that had enveloped them for so long. Emily had rejoined the group but was noticeably disturbed as her phone continued to beep with incoming texts. A frown creased her forehead as she tried to make sense out of the messages. Suddenly she announced, "Folks, it's been lovely, but I have to catch a flight. I'm needed elsewhere."

"What's wrong, Emily?" inquired Dana.

"It's probably nothing. I'll touch base with you later." And on that note, she walked out the front door.

EPILOGUE

On a sunny, picturesque beach in Southern France sits an elderly gentleman in a wheelchair. Taking no notice of the beautiful promenade filled with lovely trees and blooming flowers, his attention is focused on the shimmering sea. Even though the weather is warm, his body is wrapped in a plaid cashmere blanket. The man's hair is snow white; his body is frail and thin.

His male companion looks at him. "How are you feeling today, Rene?"

"I just need a little rest, Bernard."

"The pain, it is significant, *non*?"

"I can tolerate it. It's been an exciting life, and it won't end here. Is the plane ready for our flight this afternoon?"

Bernard lays his hand on Rene Pascal's shoulder. "Yes, we take off in a few hours. You'll be in good hands with the Swiss doctors."

Neither of the men know the Mafia and their cartels

have found Pascal and are watching for an appropriate time to kill him. They want to be certain; Pascal and his empire will no longer be a threat to their enterprise.

From a fourth-floor window where Pascal can be seen on the walkway, a man lifts his rifle and takes aim.

ACKNOWLEDGEMENTS

Writing *The Mallorcan Gambit* was a labor of love from the very beginning. When we began our writing journey, we had no idea what struggles lay ahead. One of our trio survived cancer treatments, another the death of a spouse. Our most experienced member completed a Master of Fine Arts degree at the age of eighty-seven. Overlay all of this with the COVID pandemic and its related challenges.

We are grateful to our families for giving us the time to write *The Mallorcan Gambit*, a five-year endeavor. We appreciate the patience of our publisher, Marj Charlier, as she shared her knowledge and expertise. Jeff Cacy intrigued us with stories of his visits to historical sites in Iran. *Thieves of Baghdad*, by Matthew Bogdanos, helped provide authenticity. We appreciate Beth Friedman's feedback as the first reader of our work. Granddaughter Sophia Long lent her artistic talent with our icon.

D. Marie Fitzgerald encouraged us to present *The Mallorcan Gambit* at her monthly authors series which provided useful critical input. Wendy Willson, who began as our fourth collaborator, left to develop her previously published work into a screen play. It was through Wendy that the mysterious date ranch near Joshua Tree National Park came about. Thanks also to Victoria Nelson for her advice and to Damon Prieto for nurturing us and encouraging us through hours of writing sessions along the way.

ABOUT THE AUTHORS

Judith Fabris spent most of her waking hours writing since she was in the third grade. Before *The Mallorcan Gambit,* she wrote three finance books, a money column for Copley News Service, four novels, and received an MFA in Creative Writing at the age of eighty-seven.

Sharon Prieto, a retired bank executive, has written banking articles for the local newspaper. Her desire has been to write a novel. She works tirelessly to keep us on point and is better than any of us on the computer. She loves Palm Springs and Lake Tahoe.

Donna Weeks had a long career as a teacher, adjunct professor and management consultant. She loves to write and is a grammar guru. Donna enjoyed traveling the world with her husband, Rick, and has wonderful memories of jogging through fabulous cities like Paris, Honolulu, and Singapore.